OUT OF THE MOUTH OF BABES

After I hid the boat, Penny and I ate stale sand-wiches and the mosquitoes ate us as we waited for darkness.

"We'll give it another half hour," I said.

Penny put her finger to her lips. I slipped my hand into the duffel bag and wrapped my fingers around the .38. A pair of yellow eyes stared back at me through the ferns. I eased the revolver out of the bag.

The eyes blinked and were gone. The ferns shivered.

"I vote for bobcat," I said.

Penny grinned. "Don't you just love it here?"

I said, "Aren't you scared of anything?"

The smile vanished like the yellow cat eyes.

"Not animals," the little girl said. . . .

A T.D. STASH

CRIME ADVENTURE

TOUGH ENOUGH

W.R. PHILBRICK

A SIGNET BOOK

NEW AMERICAN LIBRARY

A DIVISION OF PENGUIN BOOKS USA INC.

PUBLISHER'S NOTE

This book is a work of fiction. Names, characters, places, and incidents either are the product of the author's imagination or are used fictitiously, and any resemblance to actual persons, living or dead, events, or locales is entirely coincidental.

 SIGNET TRADEMARK REG. U.S. PAT. OFF. AND FOREIGN COUNTRIES
REGISTERED TRADEMARK—MARCA REGISTRADA
HECHO EN DRESDEN, TN

SIGNET, SIGNET CLASSIC, MENTOR, ONYX, PLUME, MERIDIAN and NAL BOOKS are published by New American Library, a divison of Penguin Books USA Inc., 1633 Broadway, New York, New York 10019

First Printing, June, 1989

1 2 3 4 5 6 7 8 9

PRINTED IN THE UNITED STATES OF AMERICA

For Nana Jean and Granny Irene
big hearts, much laughter

THE Gulf has a thousand colors, from mottled gray to luminous green, but on certain special days, at certain times, the water has no color at all. It exists as an invisible fluid that enables you to float over the sea bottom, as if suspended in air. Magic can happen then, if you let it work. Fish can walk on water, and turtles can fly.

On such a day, at such a time, a small girl with short, coppery hair cast a piece of green surgical tubing at a barracuda who wanted to dance.

"He sees it," I said. "Wind it just fast enough so it wiggles. That's good. When he hits, just keep hold of the rod with both hands."

The cuda hit the lure and ran. Line hummed like the highest note on a violin as it left the little girl's reel. I pushed on the long fiberglass pole and made *Bushwhacked* glide after the racing fish.

I said, "Lift the tip of the rod. Higher. Good. Now aim it at the fish."

I pushed some more on the pole. The little girl's father reeled in his empty line, set his expensive fly rod in the bottom of the boat, and got out a camera.

"Listen to Stash, honey," he said to the girl.

"I am, Daddy."

I said, "Keep the tip of the rod aimed at the fish

and try to reel in some line. Good. Now lift up the tip and let him dance."

The cuda came out of the water jitterbugging on his tail, trying to throw the hook. Found he couldn't and got mad enough to boogaloo.

"He's jumping!"

"That's beautiful, honey." The camera clicked.

The little girl with the zinc-white nose and the pink high-top sneakers stood on the bow of the boat and danced with fifteen pounds of rock-'n'-rolling barracuda. Pretty as a picture, the pair of them. I was as proud as her father.

"Okay. Aim the tip at the fish and reel in. See how he zigs and zags? Reel in when he zigs, let him run on the zag."

"Like that?"

"Yes. When he gets a little closer he'll see you and want to dance again. Don't fight him. Let the drag wear him out."

The cuda got an eyeful of us and tried to go airborne. He was out of gas and the line barely purred. I got down on my knees and reached over the side and took the line in by hand.

"Will he die now?" the little girl wanted to know.

"He's just tuckered."

I kept the gaff out of sight until the fish was alongside the boat, then slipped it clean into the lip. I held the big fish up beside the little girl and let her father click a few more pictures. Then I worked the hook out of the cuda's underslung jaw and set him back in the water.

"He looks sick," the little girl said. She sounded worried.

"What we'll do," I said. "We'll supercharge him."

I gripped the cuda just above the tail and yanked

it rapidly forward and back, forcing water into his gills. He began to tremble in my hands as the oxygen was restored to his depleted blood.

"Last call," I said to the fish. "You don't have to go home, but you can't stay here."

He staggered away, gaining strength with every flick of his tail. The little girl put away her spinning rod and lay facedown over the bow, shading her eyes, looking for things that lived in the turtle grass.

I poled *Bushwhacked* through the flats east of Ballast Key and tried to find bonefish for her daddy. Found, instead, a sizable tarpon feeding on a school of mullet.

"I want it," he said, stripping line from his fly rod.

"A strike will spook away any bones," I cautioned.

"Makes never no mind," he said. "I'd rather raise the tarp."

The bamboo rod began to undulate as he pumped with his right hand, feeding line with his left. His tackle was rigged for bonefish, not tarpon. The backing line was twelve-pound-test and he was casting one of Mutt's hand-tied flies. The idea was to take a fish of a size and stature to merit entry in the Key West Tournament. That is almost always the idea, but when you're using ultralight tackle on a heavyweight fighting fish, more often than not it remains simply an idea.

The tarpon, who had been lazily snacking on the mullet buffet, rolled and snapped at the fly on the second cast.

"He's on."

I kept my trap shut. The tarpon wasn't really on, he merely had the fly in his greedy mouth. Setting the hook into that hard, bony jaw was a matter of discretion and luck. That day the man had the necessary skill, but the fish had the luck. The tarpon came up, executed an insolent tap-dance over the surface of the shallow water, and spit the hook before it was set deep enough to hold. The fly fisherman sighed.

"What do ya'll think he weighed?"

I said, "Eighty or so."

"I'd say a hundred or more."

"Could be."

When it comes to questimating a fish that gets away, I tend to agree with a client. He feels better about it when the time comes to pay, and later, bellied up at the bar, the lie comes easier, and that makes him happy. A happy client makes me feel better, and the fish, wherever he frolics, the fish that got away feels best of all.

"Look, Daddy, turtles," the little girl said in a voice hushed with reverence.

In the clear, colorless water three green turtles appeared to be flying over a grass meadow of turtle grass. Gliding effortlessly through the shallows on their stubby flipper wings, as serene as levitating Buddhists. The little girl held herself motionless as she watched the turtles pass by the bow, near enough to reach out and touch. The creatures banked their flippers and circled the boat once before settling on a southwest course that would take them to a place where the sea grass was, presumably, sweeter and greener.

I heard the little girl whisper, "Good-bye turtles."

Later, at the dock, her father gave me a handsome tip on top of the half-day fee.

"You did great with her," he said. "I 'preciate it,

and I know Penny does. We wanted a special day. She lost her mama, see?"

I hadn't seen, but it explained the serious expression on a girl of eight, and the melancholy way she'd whispered good-bye to the turtles. What I did see, though, was a doting father who took the child's hand and gentled her to his side. She didn't smile, exactly, but there was plenty of spark in her pale-green eyes.

"God bless," he said as they turned to leave the dock.

Now, I ask you, does that sound like a man who would want to murder his daughter?

——— 2 ———

THE next time I saw Penny she was standing in the
doorway of Mutt Durgin's bait shack with a sky-blue
pack slung over her shoulder. I was watching the
place for Mutt, who was having a tooth pulled. I
didn't recognize the girl at first. Her hair was redder
and her legs were longer and the freckles sprayed
over her nose were more pronounced.

"Probably you don't remember," she said. "My
dad is Jake Bonner. You took us out, back in May."

She was hanging back in the doorway, waiting for
an invitation. I hauled my feet off the crab trap and
put down the paperback I'd been reading and mo-
tioned her inside.

"You hooked up with a nice little cuda," I said.

"Then you *do* remember."

It was the same voice she'd used on the turtles. I
felt honored.

"Want a soda, Penny?" I said, going to the cooler.
"Doctor Pepper or Doctor Pepper, your choice."

She accepted the bottle. Without making it too
obvious, I scanned the wharf for her father. Didn't
see him.

"So," I said, sipping from a sweating-cold bottle
of pop, "I'll bet you're down here to do some fishing, huh?"

Penny put her soda bottle down on the counter and stared at it. Stared at it hard enough to melt glass, almost. Through the window I checked out the parking lot. Still no sign of dear old dad.

"I'm running away," she said.

"Oh," I said. That explained the backpack and the lack of an accompanying parent. You see a lot of runaway kids in Key West. Most, though not all, are a few years older than Penny. Twelve or thirteen. Rarely eight, or was it nine?

"Nine," she replied, in answer to my question. "My birthday was day before yesterday."

"I'll bet your dad is worried."

"Prob'ly," she said, staring at the bottle. "I guess he'll come after me."

"You have a fight with him?"

Penny licked her lips and hugged the pack to her chest. "Not exactly," she said. She looked directly at me. "I left because I'm scared."

She unzipped the pack and fished around inside it, waiting for me to ask her what she was scared of. I asked her. She upended the pack. Banded stacks of money spilled over the counter.

"My dad wants to kill me," she said. "Is this enough money to make him stop?"

I made a telephone call, put the GONE FISHIN' sign on the door of Mutt's bait shack, and drove Penny over to Connie Geiger's place, on Eaton Street.

Connie was an old flame of mine. We'd got over being lovers, but the friendship lingered, and every now and again I enjoyed dropping by her little studio to watch her throw pots or flower vases or whatever elegant thing she happened to be shaping on the wheel. It had been the way her long fingers worked the clay that first attracted me to her. It's not every person who can be sensual with a lump of wet earth and make it into a thing of beauty.

"Connie, this is my friend Penny Bonner."

When we interrupted, Connie was applying a lime-green paint glaze to a set of salad bowls. Her hands and arms moved like a conductor urging music from an orchestra. The big propane tank was sighing as it fed heat to her kiln, situated under a shed roof behind the studio. Connie put down the bright-green brush and smiled, showing a lot of large, slightly crooked teeth.

"Hi, Penny," she said. "Here, take the end of this board and help me carry this batch out to the kiln."

I propped a hip against a bench and inhaled, enjoying the mingled scents of the clay and the paint and the aloe extract Connie used as perfume. When they returned from the shed about ten minutes later, Connie had her strong brown hand on the girl's shoulder.

"Stash," Connie said, "if you don't mind, I'd like to keep Penny around for a few days. I've got a big order to fill and can use the extra help."

"That's up to Penny."

As I'd hoped it would happen, Penny liked the idea.

"You sure it's okay?" she asked.

Connie said, "I'm sure."

With that settled, we left Connie cleaning brushes and went and sat under the fig tree in the small, shady yard behind the studio. Penny told me about her mom and her dad and Lee Ann.

"Lee Ann is my new mom," she said. "Dad and her got married on the Fourth of July."

"Do you like Lee Ann?"

"At first I did, even though it was her fault my mom died." She screwed her face up and kicked at the little piles of dirt she'd made. "Then I heard some stuff I wasn't supposed to."

"What kind of stuff did you hear, Penny?"

She hesitated and avoided making eye contact. "Just grownup stuff."

Obviously she didn't want to discuss the grown-up stuff, so I decided not to push that particular line of inquiry. "Okay," I said. "How about if you tell me why you think your dad wants to hurt you?"

Penny thought about it before answering. "First," she said, "it's not he wants to hurt me. It's he wants to *kill* me."

The word dropped like a stone between us.

"Your dad seemed like a nice guy when I met him," I said. "Why would he want to do a terrible thing like kill you?"

Penny had found a twig and was using it to scratch shapes in the dirt. Her tenseness radiated through the jagged lines she drew. " 'Cause Lee Ann said so, that's why. She said, 'Jake, like it or not, you're going to have to do something about the girl.' That's what she calls me, 'the girl,' like I don't have a name."

Penny explained that after deciding to run away she had opened her father's safe and taken what cash was there. As usual, one of her father's employees dropped her off at school. Instead of entering the schoolyard, however, she had walked ten blocks to the terminal and come down from Coral Gables by bus.

"Miss Fitzroy—she's the teacher—she'll call home to check up, but there's no one there to answer the phone but Marita, and she doesn't speak American. Lee Ann's off with Dad on business."

Assuming she was correct about her stepmother, no one would miss Penny until three o'clock, when her father or one of his employees picked her up at school. I glanced at my watch and calculated that I could have her home by three-thirty if we left within the hour. I didn't say so, but Penny guessed what I was thinking.

"I *knew* you wouldn't believe me," she said. The jagged lines in the dirt became bolts of lightning striking at her feet. "You'll meet Lee Ann and she'll sweet-talk you and then you'll prob'ly fall for her . . . just like Dad did."

She dropped the twig and tucked her hands under her arms and hugged herself. I looked down at the top of her head, where thick coppery bangs fell over her eyes. A single tear formed on the tip of her freckled nose. As I brushed it away, Penny shuddered as if the tear was made of ice.

"I'll make you a promise," I said. "I won't take you back home until you say it's okay. You can stay right here with Connie until you feel safe."

Her voice was so small and distant it might have been coming from a deep well. "You called her and told her to be nice to me, right?"

"Wrong. I called her, that's true, but there's no way I could make her be nice unless she wanted to. Not Connie."

"She doesn't really need any help."

"Penny, I know you've only just met her, but it won't take long before you'll know one thing for sure: if Connie Geiger says something, she means it."

"Okay," she said softly, "if you say so."

I wondered how overhearing her stepmother say that something should be done about her had become equated with murder in her nine-year-old mind. Whatever the real truth of the matter, I didn't want to frighten her further by expressing any doubts, not until I had a clear picture of what had really happened.

"Do me a favor," I said. "You keep that money zipped in your pack. Don't let it out of your sight. You can tell Connie about it, if you want. No one else, okay?"

Penny nodded and took a grip on the pack that left her fingertips white. I didn't mention that when the time came to return the money to her father, I wanted every bill intact for my own protection.

We had lunch, the three of us, on the porch of the conch house where Connie lived, adjacent to her studio. Cold pompano salad on a bed of lettuce. Iced tea for the adults and a glass of milk for Penny. She drank the milk to the bottom of the glass but only picked at the salad.

"How about a jelly sandwich?" Connie suggested.

"No, ma'am. It's only I'm not hungry."

I took my leave after asking Penny one last, crucial question about her mother's death, and drove back to the bait shack.

The GONE FISHIN' sign was down and the door was open. Mutt was inside, drinking rum from a paper cup and looking as mean as if he'd been chewing roofing nails and meant to spit a few in my direction.

"Damn Nazi," he said, knocking back the shot and reaching for the bottle.

"You've got me confused with someone else," I

said. "I'm the damn lazy wharf rat around here, not the damn Nazi."

"Dentist," he growled, touching his swollen jaw.

Depending on his mood, Mutt Durgin will sometimes claim to be a swamp cracker from the Everglades, but when the rum gets to him, a funny twang slips into his voice that sounds suspiciously like something you might hear along the New Jersey waterfront. He denies any such origin. All I know for sure, when he showed up in Key West he had a cussing parrot that rode his shoulder, and a gold hoop in one ear. The combination proved irresistible to camera-clicking tourists, and he made a pretty good living posing for pictures in Mallory Square until the bird got eaten by a pet alligator. Mutt tells the story better than I do—I keep forgetting exactly how it was he came by the gator-skin belt he still wears to hold up his jeans.

Nowadays he's given up the pets and the pirate earring and runs the combination bait shop and fuel dock where I keep *Bushwhacked*, my little guide boat. Mutt will book clients for me when I'm willing to work, which is as infrequently as possible.

When I started to explain my absence, he brushed aside the apology.

"T.D., I already *knowed* you was the laziest man in Key West. You 'mind me where I hid them Cubans and all is forgiven."

The Cubans he was referring to were the illicit, torpedo-shaped cigars he favored, which were becoming increasingly difficult to come by, even for a man of his nefarious connections. Some weeks before he'd hidden a few of the cigars in an old tin tackle box. I got them out and handed him one.

"Careful," I said, "it's loaded."

The cigar seemed to comfort him, or maybe it was the rum kicking in. Whatever, he puffed contentedly and the furrows on his bald, sun-mottled head smoothed out. He grinned around the cigar and held out a paper cup of the rum.

"G'wan," he said. "Be sociable."

"Can't," I said, backing out of the smoke. "I've got a date with a librarian."

3

I went home to shower. Home is a bungalow in a sleepy neighborhood in the old part of the island. It's a small, one-story job, built of cinder block laid on a slab. The tin roof is patched here and there and the white-washed stucco walls need touching up. I keep at it, but it always needs touching up. Inside, there are cool tile floors and ceiling fans. There are sun shutters on the windows and scuttles in the roof to vent the hot air. Out back there's a screened-in porch that about doubles the usable floor space—or would, if the big hammock I've rigged there didn't take up so much room. Just beyond the porch there's a small shady yard dominated by a large, thick-leaved ficus tree that tends to sigh when the wind off the Gulf is just right.

It is a small, modestly appointed place, but it is mine own.

I culled the mail from the box, transferred the circulars directly to the trash bin, and was pleased to find a money order inside a pink envelope with an Indiana postmark. The money was from a South Bend housewife whose husband had discovered that Key West was not quite the paradise he'd imagined it would be when he decided to abandon his wife and children and drink his way south. I'd found him living in the mangroves opposite Smathers Beach. "Living" is, perhaps, an exaggeration. Mr. South Bend was existing under a leaky plastic lean-to, and with all the bad rum in his blood he was on the verge of the screaming fantods when I brushed away the invisible mangrove vipers and dried him out and put him on the plane back home to Indiana.

There was a short, unsigned note enclosed with the check: "We're getting by."

A three-word novel, the story of a lifetime. Mrs. South Bend had said she'd pay me when she could; now, apparently, she could.

That unexpected check in the mail made me want to whistle. I whistled my way into the bathroom, out of my clothes, and into a pair of rubber shower thongs. There was a small green lizard in the stall when I pulled back the curtain. He stuck out his little red tongue, evidently displeased with my version of "Teddy Bears' Picnic," and vanished into a crack in the masonry when the water came on.

Believe me, an itsy-bitsy lizard in the shower is no big deal in Key West. If you live this far south—as far south as it gets in the continental U.S. of A.—you get used to coexisting with all kinds of tropical fauna. Some of them have names and talk back, like Mutt Durgin.

After the shower I brushed the pompano salad out of my teeth and slipped into clean-but-unironed cotton shorts, a clean-but-unironed cotton shirt, and a brand-new pair of the five dollar K-Mart sneakers I buy by the half-dozen. I rolled the sleeves up on the shirt, dropped a pencil stub in the pocket, and let the screen door slam behind me.

On impulse I decided to leave the coupe in the driveway and take my one-speed, just to see if it was true you never forget how to ride a bicycle.

It was true. No doubt it still is.

The Key West branch of the Monroe County Library is hot pink on the outside, and cool on the inside. The iron bars on the windows are merely decorative. You don't have to break in or out; the doors are open to the public—and to the cardholders, of which I was one.

Not that holding a card accorded me any special privilege. I still had to wait for the microfilm machine while an elderly black gentleman with a snow-white handlebar mustache cranked through the Registry of Ships. He had come all the way from Long Island, he confided, to research a pirate in the family tree.

"Great-uncle Henry claimed he was a Key West wrecker," he sighed, assembling his notebook and papers into a neat pile as he prepared to abandon the machine. "My aunt left me the silver candlesticks he said he took off the treasure ship *Clara Day* when it struck the reef in '88. I always wondered how much truth there was in the tale."

"Well?" I asked.

He shook his head and indicated the film reel. "The *Clara Day* was a guano coaster, bringing a load of birdshit up from the islands."

"Sorry," I said.

He tried to look brave, but the white mustache drooped. It was a shock to learn that Uncle Henry hadn't been an exotic species of reef pirate, but only the parlor-room variety.

I slipped into his still-warm seat. Before checking out specific dates and editions, I used the *Miami Herald* index to locate any articles that referred to Jake Bonner. There were several; most had appeared in the business section. The first, dated three years before, had focused on the rise of a handful of daring South Florida entrepreneurs, of which Bonner was the most prominent. According to the *Herald*, his chain of slick, trendy nightclubs had been started on the proverbial shoestring, with financing from venture capitalists and friends of the family. The business reporter affected a tone of bemusement that did not quite obscure a sense of middle-aged envy.

Mr. Bonner is convinced that he knows exactly what combination of style and sizzle will appeal to the 21–35 range of young adults. The first Shake'n Jake's, on the youth-oriented Fort Lauderdale strip, has met with unqualified success. As for the two new clubs that will soon open in Pompano Beach and Miami, only time will tell.

The follow-up articles and a full-blown feature in the *Sunday Herald* confirmed that time had dealt kindly with Jake Bonner and his chain of nightclubs. There were a few references to Mary Beth Bonner, his wife and the corporation's business manager, but clearly the slant was on Jake. His verve, charm, and luck. His uncanny sense of timing and entrepreneurial acumen.

It was a very different portrait of the fly fisherman I'd taken out to the flats. In the shallow waters, scanning for game fish, he'd been quiet and unassuming. No sign of the brash, inflated ego that sometimes possesses a man who has made his fortune early and with little apparent effort. If asked, I'd have guessed his occupation to be small-town lawyer or a public-school teacher. His attitude toward his daughter had been, it seemed to me, one of tender understanding. Not a bullying or domineering type—at least not when he had an Orvis fly rod in his hands.

With some sense of where Jake Bonner stood, at least in the hard-scrabble landscape of South Florida capitalism, I scrolled forward to the eleventh of March. According to Penny, her mother had died on the night of the tenth. The two-paragraph report printed the following day was not exactly studded with telling details, but I took a special interest in the name of the driver involved in the accident.

Key Largo. Mary Beth Bonner, 27, was struck and killed by a vehicle in the parking lot of a club shortly after midnight. Mrs. Bonner and her husband, Coral Gables entrepreneur Jake Bonner, were celebrating the opening of the Key Largo Shake'n Jake's, the newest in Mr. Bonner's chain of popular nightspots.

The driver of the vehicle, Lee Ann Chambers, 21, was taken into custody and released when tests for alcohol proved negative. According to the Key Largo police spokesperson, no charges have been filed at this time.

Lee Ann. Wasn't Penny's new stepmother named Lee Ann? I pushed the advance lever and watched the days blur into months until I found a brief notice in the society pages on the first Sunday in July.

Miami. Lee Ann Chambers, 21, of Miramar, married Coral Gables entrepreneur Jake Bonner, 28, in a civil ceremony. The former Ms. Chambers worked as a disc jockey in South Florida clubs. Mr. Bonner is currently developing Gator World, a family entertainment facility. The couple will reside in Coral Gables.

Maid-of-honor was Penny Bonner, 8, daughter of the groom.

It wasn't much to go on, but one thing was clear. As Penny had asserted, her stepmother had indeed been driving the car that struck her mother. That was the single, unalterable fact that must have loomed so large in her young life. The rest of it—the fear and loathing of her new mom and the resulting mistrust of her father—could be explained, I assumed, as the disturbed imaginings of a bereaved child. Considering the circumstances of her mother's death, it was only natural that Penny object to her father's new bride and invent a conspiracy that helped explain her feelings of grief and uncertainty.

There was a whole shelf of books on child psychology, but I gave them a pass. I didn't want to psychoanalyze Penny; I just wanted to help her stop being afraid. With that goal in mind, the companionship of Connie Geiger would, I hoped, be more comforting than any textbook.

I left the library reasonably content, certain I had a handle on Penny's dilemma.

Blessed are the ignorant.

4

I was shaving in a cracked mirror when the telephone rang. Smoothing my face up before going out to join the girls for dinner at the Laughing Gull. Assuming it was Connie with some last-minute request, I splashed the lather from my cheeks and went into the kitchen to pick up the phone.

It was Jake Bonner.

" 'Scuze the interruption," he drawled, after giving his name and reminding me that in May we'd fished the flats. "Thing is, we've got an emergency situation up here and I been led to believe you might be able to help."

"Pardon?" I said, glad that he couldn't see me wincing.

"My little girl run off this morning and we're pretty sure she's headed your way. To Key West, or anyhow somewheres in the Lower Keys. Natcherly I contacted the police down there, giving 'em a description and so forth. Penny's only just turned nine. I'm real concerned she's gonna get herself hurt, she gets in with the wrong crowd. Key West ain't no place for a girl her age on her own."

"No, sir," I said, adjusting the phone while I dried my semishaven face with a paper towel, "it surely isn't. Any idea what made her run away?"

Bonner sighed. "Just one of those silly misunderstandings. The girl been real confused since her momma died. What made her run don't matter. Only thing matters, we get her back safe and sound. This cop I talked to, real nice fella, said he'd put the word out, have his boys check the street kids. Other thing he suggested, I get some help from the private sector."

"I see," I said. "Was that Lieutenant Kerry you talked to, by any chance?"

"Nelson Kerry, yup. Said the best man for the job was a lazy, no-good fishing guide by the name of T. D. Stash. Imagine my surprise. That right, Stash, you do a little moonlighting for runaway kids?"

"Not only kids," I said. "Anyone in trouble."

"Cop said if Penny showed anywhere between Big Pine and Key West you'd find her. Hell, I told him, she'll prob'ly come knockin' on his door, seein' as how he's the only individual she knows in Key West."

I cleared my throat and felt my face getting hot. "Your daughter was only on the boat the one time," I said. "I'm surprised she'd remember me."

He explained that I'd made a strong impression on his daughter and that for weeks after she'd talked excitedly about catching and releasing the barracuda and seeing the green turtles.

"Hell," Bonner said with a friendly good-old-boy inflection, "got so's I was a little jealous of you myself, all the time hearin' 'Stash said this' and 'Stash did that.' So when the man at the bus station told us he'd sold a Key West ticket to a girl looked a lot like the picture we showed 'im, I natcherly thought of you. Hearin' the cop recommendation only con-

27

firms my first instinct. I figure it oughta be easy for you to locate her—it ain't that big an island."

"Sometimes it gets tricky," I said. "Especially with kids."

"Then you'll hire on to find her?"

There was no avoiding it. For that matter, it was only the promise I'd made to Penny that prevented me from relieving his anxiety right then. But my big mouth had got me in a delicate situation—and not for the first time.

"Sure," I said. "The way it works, I usually go through a lawyer friend of mine. That gives us a legal structure and affords me some protection. What you do is retain the lawyer and the lawyer hires me."

"Sounds reasonable," he said. "What kind of fee you need?"

I explained about the sliding scale, depending on how much the client could afford, and how there were other factors that had to be taken into account: personal expenses, the duration of the search, the difficulty of a locating a particular individual. Mostly I was stalling for time, uneasy about the idea of establishing a fee that might, after the fact, be construed as exploitive, considering the fact that I already knew exactly where his daughter could be found.

While I hemmed and hawed, Bonner volunteered a sum that broke my chain of thought.

"That's about four times the usual," I said when I had my breath back.

"I wanted to get your attention."

"You got it. Let me put it this way, Mr. Bonner—"

"Jake, please."

"Okay, Jake. If you're right about Penny coming

to my door, the fee won't be anywhere near that much, okay?"

He chuckled. "You don't want my money, I ain't gonna argue. Thing is, I'm real worried. It ain't only that she run away. Hell, a lot of kids do that, I did it myself once or twice. It's the fact she's got two thousand in cash with her."

I managed to feign surprise as he explained about finding the cash missing from his safe.

"You know as well as I do," he said, "somebody down there'd kill her for a tenth of that."

"Any idea why she took so much money?"

"Tryin' to get my attention, I guess. Like I tried to get yours."

I gave him Lil Cashman's office number and explained that she was my attorney in such matters and would handle the necessary paperwork.

"That's all fine," he said, "just so's we find her quick. By the way, I sent one of my boys down to the Key West police with copies of her picture. He should be there anytime now."

I made noises of assurance, concluded the conversation, and hurried out the door.

The coupe was buried under fallen palm fronds. After clearing them off the hood and out of the front seat, I got all eight cylinders firing and eased the big-finned Caddy through the narrow streets, resisting the impulse to step on the gas and hurry it along.

I was somewhat dismayed to find Penny sitting on Connie's front steps, in full view of anyone who cared to look. She, in turn, was taken aback when I hustled her inside the shop.

"It's low-profile time," I said, trying to make light

of my haste. "Just for the heck of it we're going to eat in tonight. I'll phone the Laughing Gull for takeout."

No doubt I was overreacting. The possibility that Jake Bonner's emissary might spot Penny on his way to the police station was slim. More worrisome was the chance that Lieutenant Kerry's men might immediately circulate the girl's picture to the neighborhood.

"Is there a problem?" Connie wanted to know.

She came out of her bedroom barefoot, wearing white slacks and a gauzy Indio print blouse tied under her breasts, showing off the slight, feminine curve of her belly and an intriguing navel that was as deep as the imprint of a sculptor's thumb. Magenta lipstick matched the highlights on her blouse. Red feathered earrings showed where she'd swept back her thick mop of jet-black hair. If the effort was for me, I appreciated it, although Connie didn't require ornaments or cosmetics to make herself attractive. Her style glowed from the inside.

"Just a slight hitch in plans," I said, and explained about Penny's picture being delivered to the police.

Penny's reaction was to huddle herself in a wicker rocking chair and tuck her knees under her chin. She looked terrified, and I was again reminded that it was fear—imagined, or not—that had compelled her to leave home. I felt better about keeping my promise.

"No one is going to hurt you here," I said, kneeling beside the rocker. "You just keep yourself out of sight for a couple of days and we'll straighten everything out."

"It's Lee Ann. She's the one made him do it. *She's* the one."

Connie made a soft, clucking sound and took the

frightened girl onto her lap. For a moment, as they rocked, Penny looked several years younger.

So, for that matter, did Connie.

I sat at the Laughing Gull tiki bar and nursed a draft beer, waiting for a takeout order of conch fritters, chips, and steamed corn. Attempting, as I gazed out at the crepuscular quiet of the inner harbor, to expiate a nagging sense of inadequacy.

"The same again," I said when the barmaid came around.

I wasn't cut out to play hero for nine-year-old girls. Or for anybody else, for that matter. So I'd done what nonheroic types do, if they can: I'd dumped trouble in the lap of a trusted friend.

The barmaid rubbed a damp rag over the counter and sidled close.

"Hey, T.D., you okay?"

"Sure I'm okay."

"You look a little peaked."

I put a grin on and said, "It's my pointy little head and my beetle brows."

She relaxed and put away the damp rag. "Mutt was in earlier. Had to shut him off. He got it fixed in his mind that one of the German tourists was a Nazi dentist. I go to him, 'Mutt, the poor guy is here on vacation, all he wants to do is eat his oysters in peace, give him a break.' But you know Mutt."

"Deed I do."

"One of the busboys walked him back to his trailer."

"He'll appreciate that," I said, "if he remembers."

A tour boat cleared the breakwater, setting out for the sunset cruise around the island. There were people lined along the rails, staring into the amber twilight. Perhaps one of them was the German tourist, making good his escape from Mutt Durgin.

I thought about putting Connie and Penny aboard a boat and sending them off to the Marquesas. They could camp under the stars and keep an eye peeled for green turtles while I checked out Jake Bonner and his new wife and his empty safe. It was only an impractical daydream, but it would come back to haunt me with cold nightmare sweats.

Maybe it was the draft beer, or the sun going down, or the sense of uneasiness left over from the conversation with Penny's father. Whatever the reason, I'd lost my appetite by the time the order was ready.

"You guys chow down," I said after lugging the stuff back to Eaton Street and setting the takeout cartons on Connie's kitchen counter. "I'm going over to blow smoke at the heat."

Penny had settled down. The red was gone from her eyes and she was smiling, tentatively. "What's he mean, Connie?"

"Ignore him," Connie advised, "he's about to go away."

The coupe took up two of the parking slots in back of the station house. One of the slots was reserved for Nelson Kerry, so I assumed, correctly, that he was off-duty. Detective Sergeant Sawyer had taken charge of the second shift. He didn't know me, and he resisted the idea that Detective Lieutenant Kerry and I were the best of friends.

"Never heard Nel mention any T. D. Stash," he said, puffing on a briar pipe.

"We go way back, Sergeant. It was my tricycle he

was riding when he chipped his tooth. I was the one poured ink in his lunchbox."

Puff, puff. "The lieutenant didn't leave any instructions regarding his schoolboy chums."

"We used to trade baseball cards. He still owes me a Whitey Ford."

The pipe gurgled and the sergeant smiled ever so slightly. "Maybe what you should do," he said, "you should file a complaint."

He wanted me to act humble. I played along, ducking my head and saying "Gosh, Sarge, really?" and eventually he went out to the desk and came back with the typed instructions Kerry had left concerning distribution of the Xerox color prints of Penny Bonner.

"You can get these run off from a slide," he said, handing me a copy of the picture.

"Gosh, Sarge, really?"

"Cut it out."

I was pleased to see that the Xerox transfer had made Penny's hair color unreal and missed the freckles altogether. The likeness was there if you looked for it, but it required more concentration than the average citizen of Key West was likely to exert on just another runaway kid.

"You talk to the man who delivered these?"

Sawyer shook his head.

"What kind of orders did the lieutenant issue regarding the missing girl?"

Sawyer shook his head again. "I'm not obliged to tell you that."

"Gosh, Sarge, real—"

The butt of the pipe clanged against the ashtray.

"The flier is being posted in the usual places," he said, staring at the pipe as if it had betrayed him.

33

"Each squad car has a copy, and the officers have been instructed to keep an eye out for a girl fitting the description. They may or may not remember, depending on how crazy it gets on Duval Street."

I put the Xerox version of Penny in my shirt pocket, thanked the sergeant, and left. In the parking lot a tow-truck driver was just about to slip the hook into the coupe. He let me go when I explained that I was Charles Manson, out on bail.

5

LILY Cashman lives in a southside, seaside condo. After a couple of drinks she will sing that for you, make it a catchy mambo tune. "*South* side *sea* side, let's dance to the condo beat." There are uniformed security guards in the chromed and mirrored lobby. There are sauna rooms, tennis and handball courts, and a male concierge named Adolfo who will arrange the delivery of anything legal, including fresh caviar, providing your MasterCard isn't over the limit. There is, no surprise, a waiting list, and an unspoken assumption that residence be restricted to gay tenants.

Lily's third-floor balcony overlooks an artificial beach. The white sand on top was trucked down from the Carolinas. The lumpy, off-color stuff underneath was pumped in from offshore. The rows of coconut palms were imported from Jamaica and cleverly wired in place to withstand the strong, steady tug of the trade winds. At night the palms are illuminated from spotlights buried in the sand, and the green fronds look like the stiff skirts of Degas ballerinas.

It is not my idea of home sweet home, but Lily likes it and I like Lil. Some of the things I like about her are physical. The auburn hair going sun-blond at the ends. The slim, high-breasted figure. The lime-green eyes. The great ass. She's exactly my type, but, alas, there is no reciprocal spark. From Lil's point of view, I'm the wrong gender. Her heart belongs to Samantha, a diminutive beach urchin with dark eyes and a wild, partytime laugh.

Lil was waiting at her door, having been warned by security about the approach of an unkempt individual wearing discount sneakers. Her evening attire was confined to a crisp white man-size dress shirt.

"Sami's down in the weight room," she said, handing me a Kirin beer. "She's been down there every night, fucking with the Nautilus machine."

"Oh," I said. To an interested observer their relationship seemed to be based on love, affection, and argument, not necessarily in that order.

"Sam says it's very important to build up her strength so she can win the 'round-island race."

"What do you think is important?" I asked, staring at the dragon on the beer label.

"I dunno," Lil said, pacing her long, lightly tanned legs over the white carpet. "I've never been jealous of an exercise machine. This is a new experience."

We went out to the balcony. I sat in a molded-plastic chair while she leaned against the rail and blew smoke from her nose, just like the mythical beast on the beer label. I told her part of the story, the part about Jake Bonner hiring me to find his daughter. I neglected to mention that his daughter had found me first.

"Shake'n Jake, huh? You ever been to one of his clubs?"

"Can't say I have."

Lily shrugged. "Neon flamingos, potted palms, lots of chrome. Very *Miami Vice*. The one we were at, up in Miramar, had a sound system would shake the fillings from your teeth."

"Sounds like fun."

"Oddly enough, it was. Okay, so a kid has run away from home and you've promised to find her. I'll draw up the standard contract." Lil gave me a lawyerish squint, the kind that is supposed to make you speak the truth, or at least squirm. "It sounds pretty routine, T.D. Why the brooding, worried look?"

"Let's just say the domestic situation leaves something to be desired."

"It usually does, if a kid takes off. What's so special about the Bonner household?"

It was a tricky thing, feeding Lil Cashman a selective version of the truth, but I knew I was on shaky legal ground and didn't want to compromise her any more than was necessary to ensure Penny's safety.

"There's a question of abuse," I said, hedging.

Her eyebrows became inverted V's. "Sexual abuse?"

"Not that I'm aware of," I said. "Emotional neglect is more like it."

The breeze was playing an interesting game with the tail of her shirt, and she caught me looking. "Wash your mind out with soap, you nasty boy. Let's get back on track. I'm guessing, but I think your problem is you want to know if you'll be obliged to return the child to her father, assuming you locate her."

"Is there an alternative?"

"There's always an alternative. If the child will testify to an abusive or disrupted home situation, you can turn her over to the social service and let them handle it."

"Ouch," I said. "The very thought."

"There are good people working for the bureau, if

you can cut through the red tape and the bullshit. Caring people."

"Well," I said, prying myself loose from the plastic seat, "I guess I better find the kid first, right?"

Lil gave me that lie-detector squint again and said, "Sure, you do that."

I was just about to leave when Sam returned from her fling with the Nautilus machine. She had showered and her hair smelled of aloe when I bent down to nuzzle the top of her head.

"Hey, handsome"—she grinned—"you make a pass at my girl?"

"Of course," I said.

That night I slept in the hammock, suspended in the dry, tepid air. The ficus tree sighed and whispered. The palm fronds made a noise like summer rain, and the moths played a soft, dreamy blitzkrieg against the screen. As I nodded off, the conversation with Jake Bonner kept replaying in my head. Each time it ran through I listened, hoping he would call his daughter by name.

"The girl," he kept saying, "the girl been real confused since her momma died."

When I awoke, my mouth tasted of moth. I lay in the hammock until I could smell coffee fumes wafting from the little bodega on the corner. After a quick, cold shower I put on a pair of pressed slacks and a new Lacoste shirt and a pair of polished toe pinchers. A costume designed to impress the quality folks in Coral Gables.

The Cuban coffee from the bodega was hot and sweet. I sipped from the paper cup as the coupe settled into a groove on the Overseas Highway, heading up through the hundred-mile string of islands to the mainland.

"It's Lee Ann," Penny had insisted. "She's the one made him do it."

The refrain fit into the bump-and-grind rhythm of fat whitewall tires hitting imperfections in the road. My old Coupe de Ville is not exactly a thing of beauty. The upholstery is slashed, the trunk lid is rust-blistered from transporting salt-drenched fishing gear, and the muffler has a chronic cough. Never mind. The cruise control works, the big, thirsty V-8 has power to spare, and the stereo will blow your hair back even when the convertible top is up.

I slipped a Sade cassette into the deck and let her windswept voice wash over me while the Caddy ate up the miles. In the tentative, early-morning light the shallows of the Gulf were a luminous shade of milky green. The mangrove keys seemed to hover above the water, like small, compressed clouds.

Sade whispered that I was a smooth operator. I wasn't so sure. The tight leather shoes made my feet hurt and I hadn't the vaguest idea what to say to Jake Bonner, when and if I saw him.

" 'Scuze me, bub, is it true you murdered your wife?"

Or maybe a little more subtlety was in order.

"Hey, speaking of coincidence, I hear you married the woman who ran over your wife. Small world, huh?"

Before leaving the island I'd stopped by to check on Penny. She was asleep on a futon that had been laid out beside Connie's bed. Her fists were balled up and her eyelids were fluttering. Fighting something in her sleep. Connie had given me a grave, quiet kiss on the lips and told me the plan was to keep Penny so busy she wouldn't have time to worry.

"She's a sweet kid," Connie said. "Someone has hurt her, but I don't think there's any permanent damage. Not yet."

Not yet . . . I know a thing or two about not yet. Not yet can come back to nip your ankles or soil the rug. If it isn't correctly disciplined, it can go for the throat like a pit bull on speed. I wanted to get Penny back with her family, but there was something about the way Jake Bonner had handled me over the phone that made me uneasy.

Before I broke my promise, I wanted to look him in the eye. I wanted to hear him call his daughter by name.

In Coral Gables the Haitians had landed. There was a Haitian raking the bleached marble chips along the long, curving path up to the house. There were two Haitians trimming grass near the canal wall, and another adjusting the fiberglass whips that kept the new Rybovich 55 from bumping the dock.

I'd left the coupe a few blocks away and walked, just to get a feel for the neighborhood. When the white gravel crunched under my feet, the Haitians stopped moving, as if trying to blend into the sun-drenched landscape. Any strange white face might belong to an Immigration agent. I tried to look harmless, but the yard workers weren't buying any. They had the look of thin black herons about to take flight.

The Bonner residence was a sprawling thing of white stucco and smoked glass. The red roof tiles made it look like the house was wearing a corrugated party hat. A Haitian woman opened the front door and waited for me to speak. The intervening screen made it difficult to see her face, but even in shadow I could tell she was as thin as the menfolk toiling in the yard.

"Is Mr. Bonner at home?"

Behind the dark screen a red scarf moved as she shook her head.

"How about Mrs. Bonner? Tell her it's about her stepdaughter, Penny."

The door closed. I waited, scuffing my new shoes on the mosaic inlaid into the front steps. A few minutes later the door opened and the black woman unlocked the screen. I followed her inside, down a cool tiled hallway, and out to a glass-enclosed veranda that overlooked the canal.

Lee Ann Bonner was standing behind a glass-topped table, where she was arranging hibiscus blossoms in a cut-crystal vase. She was wearing a black tank top, black Capri pants, and her feet were bare. On first impression she looked to be a leggy blond teenager who'd just gotten her braces off and was uncertain of her smile.

"I thought you'd be the police," she said.

The silky, confident voice did away with the first impression. The smile was tentative rather than uncertain. Ready to vanish if the news was bad. When I told her who I was, the smile stayed.

"So you're the man from Key West," she said, extending her right hand. "The fishing guide Penny had such a crush on. Have you found her?"

I trotted out the story I'd prepared on the drive up. "There's some kids crashing at an old campsite on Stock Island. I think Penny may be hanging out with them."

"So she's okay?"

"Haven't seen her with my own eyes," I said, deciding that Lee Ann was either a genuine towhead blond, or else she took the trouble to dye her eyelashes. "The kids have a habit of vanishing into the mangroves if a stranger gets too near. What I need to know, Mrs. Bonner, is what made her decide to run away. If I know that, maybe I can figure a way to coax her into the open."

I thought it was a great little story. The pale-blue, almond-shaped eyes looked me over, registering wariness and then deciding to cooperate. Lee Ann slipped the last of the hibiscus blossoms into the vase and asked Marita to bring out a pitcher of iced tea. That startled me. I hadn't realized the maid was still on the veranda.

"Have a seat," Lee Ann said. "I'm just going to wash my hands."

There was a sink at the bar. She scrubbed with the economic thoroughness of a surgeon.

"I'm afraid it's my fault," she said, running her cupped hands under the water. "I opened my big mouth and said something I shouldn't have."

When Marita returned with the tea, I saw that her face was as immobile as a ritual mask. Her cheeks were high and pockmarked. Smallpox scarring is not that unusual among the Haitian poor, but the trace of the ancient disease makes clearing immigration especially difficult. I wondered what employment agency Jake Bonner used, or if he just drove the big Rybovich over to Haiti and took them off the beach.

"I understand Penny's mother died," I said, pouring tea into two chilled, ice-filled glasses. "Has she had any emotional problems?"

"Some, naturally," Lee Ann said. She added sugar to the tea and a slice of lime from the tray. "Like I was saying, though, her biggest problem has been me. Accepting me."

"Jealous of her dad's attention?"

"Not exactly. The problem is her mother died in a car accident. She was run over. I was driving the car."

I tried to look startled.

"I know it sounds bizarre. It *was* bizarre." Lee Ann sat on a chaise longue, tucking her feet under her bottom, a position that would have cracked my spine. She made it look comfortable. "I was auditioning as a disc jockey down there in Key Largo. Working the Shake'n Jake circuit is good money— better than what I was making at 'PIX, this low-watt station—so I was nervous. Not too nervous, though, because I got through the set without making a fool of myself, and the manager said it was fine. The idea is you keep 'em dancing they'll get thirsty and buy drinks, which I guess they did. So when I packed up my stuff and left, I was on top of the world. Thought I'd get the job, no problem. So I'm driving this rented car, okay? Assumed I had the headlights on, only maybe I didn't. No one was really sure about that afterward. What happened is, Mary Beth crossed out from between two parked cars and I never saw her."

"Was Penny there when it happened?"

The blond bangs shimmered as she shook her head. "Thank the Lord, no. She was home in bed. It was pretty awful to look at, what the car did to her mom. What *I* did to her. You know the really weird thing? This is terrible. It was their anniversary. The seventh."

"Bad luck," I said.

"I felt so horrible, you know? So guilty. I was at

43

the inquest, which is this cold, formal kind of thing, and the little girl was there with her father and I just didn't know what to do. I couldn't hide from those little green eyes. So what I did, finally, I went over and gave the little girl a hug and told her how sorry I was. Which is a pretty pathetic thing to say when you've been responsible for the death of a parent. Even though it wasn't my fault, technically. I was expecting maybe she'd hit me or something—I mean, could you blame her? But she just gave me this incredible look and said, 'Mommy's an angel now.' "

"And that's how you met Jake?"

"Well, I met him right after the accident, of course, but that doesn't count. He was in shock, he didn't know who I was."

Lee Ann stirred the tea by swirling the ice cubes. A powerboat went by in the canal. All I could see was the flying bridge and the teenage boy at the controls. He was going fast enough to leave a sizable wake, which explained the elaborate mooring whips to keep the million-dollar Rybovich from grinding against the dock.

"You probably don't believe in love at first sight," Lee Ann said. "I sure didn't. What a dumb idea. Only that's what happened with me and Jake, there at the inquest, the first time we really got a look at each other. And it was all because of Penny. Because she said just the right thing. Instead of being mad, she was very sweet to me and I looked at Jake and he looked at me and it happened, just like that. I just melted, you know?"

I didn't know. I couldn't even imagine. I'd never run over anyone and then fallen in love with the surviving spouse, just like that. I could imagine falling for Lee Ann, though, no trouble at all. Everything about her was attractive. Which reminded me what Penny had said: "She'll sweet talk you and then you'll prob'ly fall for her, just like Dad did."

Dear old Dad. I asked Lee Ann where Jake was.

"Poor Jake," she said. "It made him sick not to be able to stay here at home, waiting for news, but he had to go to the site. No way around it. There's these investment bankers down from Boston, and a survey crew, and there was just no way he could get out of it."

"I'm sorry," I said. "The site?"

"Gator World. Or what's going to be Gator World, one of these days. It's Jake's new thing. It's right off the Tamiami Trail, which makes it a super location. Anyhow, he's over there with the bank people."

"I'll catch him later. You've helped a lot, Lee Ann. But was there anything specific that happened prior to Penny running away? Anything I can use, if I get close enough to talk with her?"

Lee Ann nodded. The pale, gold-flecked blue eyes were like warm lanterns. They made me feel sleepy and content.

"She heard me tell Jake I was pregnant. I'm going to have a baby. A little girl."

———————— *6* ————————

I spent all of that day, and part of the next, doing what an unlicensed troublemaker does best: sticking my nose where it doesn't belong, disturbing sleeping dogs.

Poking around.

There were two things that still needed poking after my chat with Lee Ann. One was the *Miami Herald*, the other was Jake Bonner. The traffic heading downtown convinced me to try Bonner first and leave the bayside paper for midafternoon.

You can't miss the Tamiami Trail, also known as Route 43. It runs clear across the top of Coral Gables. All north–south roads in the Greater Miami area intersect the Tamiami. Which made it, as Lee Ann had said, a super location for a tourist attraction. I drove west on it through the congested, bleached-white suburbs, stopping at stoplights like a good little citizen.

There were thunderheads building in the sky, but I left the top down and the stereo up. Wanting to share my latest musical discovery with everyone in range. "Night Birds," by a harmonic genius named Edward Gerhard, who somehow managed to get symphonic sound from an unamplified six-string guitar. Judging by the number of disapproving glares I collected, most of my fellow travelers were tone-deaf.

The suburbs began to peter out, giving way to the damp flatlands of the Everglades. The horizon-wide river of saw grass and shallow water that has been poked and prodded by civilization, drained and dammed by the Army Corps of Engineers. Lately it has become a great, swampy stage where environmentalists prophesy doom. Lurking just behind the scenery, developers sharpen their survey stakes and eye that fattest of fattened calfs: the bottom line. Meanwhile, implacable and ancient, the glades live on. For the time being.

Twenty or so miles into the flatlands I saw a big, plywood alligator floating just over the horizon. Only in South Florida. It was, of course, a billboard.

Future Site of Jake Bonner's
GATOR WORLD
Excitement & Adventure for the Whole Family

I had trouble finding the access road. Mostly because it wasn't really a road yet. It was a crude, back-filled path that went straight into the upper limits of the vast, soggy area where the Everglades meld into the Big Cypress Swamp. The dirt path was maybe six feet above the average water level. No doubt Bonner intended to pave it over, if he could raise enough money from the Yankee investment bankers. Until then, maximum speed in a low-slung Coupe de Ville was ten miles per, which meant it took almost forty-five minutes to reach the isolated construction site.

Portions of it loomed over the flat, saw-grass horizon, visible from more than a mile away. The concrete spires of an unfinished amusement ride, possibly a water slide. There wasn't enough of it done to be sure.

The rutted path intersected with a crude, thirty-acre rectangle of backfill. The parking area, eventually. Bonner was thinking big. Just finishing the access road and paving the lot would require a not-so-small fortune. The ticket booths were already in place. Adjacent to the lot was a much larger, man-made island. Maybe a hundred acres. Skeletal structures of futuristically shaped architecture jutted up out of the fill, raw and unfinished. Foundation pads had been laid for a massive entrance, tied to a partially completed geodesic dome that would have Buckminster Fuller spinning like a dervish in his grave.

There were only two vehicles in the huge parking area. A black El Camino pickup with tinted windows and a metallic-red Porsche. The vanity plates on the Porsche read SHAKEN-J.

I pulled in next to the pickup and sat there for a couple of minutes, admiring the man's audacity. Gator World wasn't just another roadside attraction, as I'd first assumed, but a thing writ large against the landscape, on the scale of a minor Disneyland. Completing it would take more millions than I could count on all my fingers and toes. A whole lot more.

The dust the coupe had kicked up had just about settled when a helicopter exploded upward from behind the geodesic dome. It circled over the bare steel spires and then accelerated east. Heading, I assumed, for Miami International Airport.

Departing bankers, perhaps. I wondered what they had concluded, after an inspection of the actual site. Did they intend to buy the dream? If so, they could make it as real as anything else man had devised in South Florida. If not, Jake Bonner might well be trading in the Porsche for something a tad more economical.

I got as far as the big dome. That was when Swamp Thing stepped out from behind a concrete piling and made threatening noises.

"Yo begoff, nawantah har," it said.

"You back off, you're not wanted here" would be a rough translation.

I might have understood sooner, except I had to blink and rub my eyes, convinced I was seeing double. There were two Swamp Things. Both large and hairy, with pale-blue eyes and bad teeth. Both aiming Colt Python .38s at my midsection.

Ellis and Orrin Cullen. The bad-news twins. That was how I first made their acquaintance. It was the start of a beautiful friendship that seemed to revolve around them pointing guns, mostly at me.

"Easy now, boys, he don't look like no bird-watcher."

Jake Bonner came out of the dome. He was wearing a spiffy white linen suit with an ice-green silk tie. There were little alligators on the tie. There may have been clocks on his socks, but I was too busy watching the goons with the guns to check it out.

"You better state yer name and business," Bonner suggested, smiling amiably. "Help clear up this misunderstanding."

I thought of a smart remark, but decided the twins might be insulted by words of more than one syllable. To his credit, Jake Bonner appeared vexed and embarrassed when he finally recognized me.

"T. D. Stash. Son of a bitch. I didn't expect to see you here." He came forward and gripped my hand. The Cullen brothers, who he then introduced, holstered their weapons. They didn't look the least bit apologetic. "How it is, we been hassled by this group of activists from the Audubon Society," Bonner explained. "Claim the enterprise is gonna endanger the habitat for all the flyin' critters. They been in here takin' pictures and they got a temporary injunction against us, so Ellis and Orrin are kinda edgy, you know?"

I knew about edgy. I also knew about menacing thugs. They were not a pair I would have chosen as a welcoming committee for impressionable financiers. Maybe they had managed to keep out of sight, like most of the creatures spawned by the great swamp.

"Come on inside," Bonner said. "Lee Ann called me on the cellular phone, said you'd located Penny for us. That's good news."

We entered the dome. The Cullens stayed outside. Not housebroken, apparently. Inside, a portion of the dome had been enclosed with plastic panels and turned into a promotional display. This was where the Yankee bankers had been entertained, if the empty champagne bottles were any indication. Light and power were provided by a portable generator that made a nagging sound, like the whine of a mosquito.

"This is what she'll look like, by and by," Bonner said.

He threw a switch, illuminating an architectural model of the theme park as it would appear when completed. The water slides had little human figures in place, frozen in aspects of aquatic delirium. There were to be a whole series of geodesic domes. Several were cut away to show the interior displays. The largest was called "Night of the Living Swamp," a gator-filled replica of a primeval swamp. There was a mini-domed screening room, where something called *The Age of Alligators* was about to be shown. There were retail stores for leather products and souvenirs, and a series of interlocking canals, brimming with little plastic gators. There was a riverboat excursion through a jungle thick with Spanish moss and vines, and an airboat thrill ride called "Jaws of Death."

"Later on we'll have on-site hotel facilities," Bonner said. "Package deals with all the major airlines. We're looking at a potential first-season attendance in the low seven figures, minimum."

"I'm impressed," I said. As I eyeballed the fancy model, it was easy to forget that so far Gator World was mostly a giant, unpaved parking lot in the middle of a sea of saw grass and sunlight.

"About the girl," Bonner said. "Can you lay hands on her? Is she okay?"

I repeated my story about Penny being spotted at a campground on Stock Island.

Bonner nodded, his eyes never leaving my face.

"The poor kid is prob'ly homesick by now," he said. "It been a rough eight months for the both of us. I gotta say, though, she couldn't a picked a worse time for a stunt like this."

"How so?"

He gestured at the model. "We're at a crucial point, regarding the enterprise. Financing is in place, but we've got us a few hurdles to clear. Legal hurdles. Them activists I mentioned, they got the Audubon and the Sierra Club on my back, taking us to court. Like I said, they slapped on a temporary injunction, forbidding we continue construction. We'll be in court starting next week, for appeal. I been so wound up here, it appears I ain't paid sufficient attention to the girl."

"And that's why she took the money and ran away, to get your attention?"

51

Bonner loosened his tie. "Partly," he said. "Partly it's other things. We're having what they call a difficult period of adjustment, the three of us. Lee Ann, the girl, and me. Thing is, she still pines for her mom, which I don't hardly blame her. I do, too. But we got to get on with things, don't we? It ain't like it was Lee Ann's fault, what happened to Mary Beth. It was fate. Fate what killed Mary Beth, fate what brought Lee Ann and me together."

I nodded solemnly. Jake Bonner sounded like a man who made a religion of fate, and I saw no point in expressing any doubts in that faith or the future of his ambitious "enterprise."

"Come on out here and see what we already got built," he said, turning me away from the model.

We exited the dome into the sunlight. A walkway had been laid in new asphalt. It led to another series of interlocking domes. There were steel pens set up alongside the walkway. A peculiar musky odor exuded from the pens. Eau d'alligator.

"We callin' it Gator World, and that means we need lots of gators," Jake said, pausing to rest his forearm against one of the pens. "Ellis and Orrin been a big help, rounding 'em up. Buying 'em off dealers. The idea is, we'll breed 'em here. The goal is to have a thousand or more healthy gators. Last count we had about four dozen full growed and a whole lot of young'uns."

The gators were ambling sluggishly through the narrow pens, blinking in the sunlight. They looked, as they always did to me, slightly insolent. Full of slow, reptilian contempt for all mammals—and two-legged types in particular.

"Cute little devils, ain't they?" Bonner said, grinning.

"Adorable," I said. "This seems like a long way from the disco, Jake."

He nodded. "Damn straight it is. I'll tell you a little secret, T.D. The Shake'n Jake chain is makin' money hand over fist, but the thrill is gone. I did what I set out to, regarding them clubs. Now I got the leverage to bust through to the next level. Which we got a taste of right here."

He pushed through steel-jacketed doors into the connected domes. I followed and was instantly disoriented by the darkness.

Jake chuckled and grabbed hold of my elbow. "Take a few minutes to get used to. Then you'll see plenty."

I stumbled along, feeling steel grates vibrating to my footsteps. Gradually the gloom became discernible. We were on a catwalk above a dank, spooky-looking swamp. The dome structures that enclosed it formed a kind of night sky, complete with faintly illuminated stars.

"I'll brighten her up some," Jake offered.

He went to a power grid and snapped a few switches. The lights came up slightly and I could see to the distant edges of the exhibit, where a full-scale diorama mural contributed to the illusion that the swamp didn't cease at the dome walls. The catwalk spanned the place, which had the volume of a good-sized aircraft hangar. Jake insisted that we walk into the middle area, so we could "get the swampy feeling" and see the full effect of the exhibit.

" 'Course, we ain't introduced the wildlife yet," he said, "except for a few of them noisy tree frogs that found their way inside, and a snake or two. I had creek beds dug out, like you see there, and deeper areas for gator holes. The water that trickles through is genuine Everglades, diverted by conduit. The saw grass is real—hell, the place was thick with it when we started the backfill—but every single one of them trees is handmade from fiberglass. Even the leaves are plastic.''

That surprised me. The thick stands of cypress, strewn with Spanish moss, looked utterly convincing. We might have been in the backwaters of the Big Cypress Swamp, except that the dim, humid atmosphere was noticeably free of mosquitoes.

"The trees cost me a fortune, but they're worth it. The idea is, we'll make it as near to a real nighttime swamp as money can buy. Real gators, real birds, snakes, possum. A few small deer. All doin' what they do best, which is blend into the swamp. Folks'll come in here blinkin' like you did, and at first they'll see mostly nothing but cypress and swamp grass. They'll think Jake Bonner has cheated 'em. Then, as their eyes adjust, they'll start to pick out a few gator snufflin' around them gator holes. Then they'll see that long-legged bird tryin' to look like a tree branch, and the snakes writhin' through the moss. After a while they'll realize the swamp is teeming with exotic wildlife. Leave 'em dazed and amazed, that's my motto.''

I was a little of each by the time we exited "Night of the Living Swamp." The blinding sunlight contributed to my sense of confusion. Jake Bonner had diverted me back a few thousand years and it wasn't easy returning to the present. I concentrated on Penny, on her inarticulate fear, and that helped. As Jake walked me back to my car, I tried to get a few things straight.

"Penny blames Lee Ann for her mother's death," I said. "Is that fair to say?"

His head bobbed. I noticed that his hair, cut fashionably short, was almost as white-blond as Lee

Ann's. It was difficult to tell in the direct sunlight, but it looked like a faint patch of freckles spanned the bridge of his nose, just like Penny's. The mouth, though, was different. Harder, less expressive. Maybe Penny had her mother's mouth.

"I guess she does blame her," Bonner said. He stroked the silk tie absently and dropped his gaze to the ground. "I know it was Lee Ann drivin' the vehicle, but it weren't her fault. Except I can't make the girl understand. I thought everything was okay between them, only it must be Penny was keeping her feelings bottled up inside. She was spouting a whole lot of crazy nonsense before she run off. Lee Ann thinks she jealous of the new baby that's coming." He lifted his eyes and looked at me, unblinking. "You think that could be it?"

It was unsettling, looking into those ultra-pale-blue eyes. They made me want to tell the truth, and that was always dangerous.

"I don't know, Jake. When Penny's back home you'll have to ask her."

In the vast unfinished parking lot the Cullen brothers leaned against the El Camino pickup and stared at me with cross-hair eyes as I walked to the coupe and left, leaving a rooster tail of marl dust hanging in the sunlight.

7

IN Miami I steered the coupe into a gas station, left instructions that the tank be filled, and then fed coins into a pay phone. The number rang for a while. When Connie answered, she explained that she and her new assistant had been out at the kiln, overseeing a glaze.

"Penny's been a big help," she said. "She has enthusiasm, energy, and she's smart as a whip."

"Glad to hear it."

"You won't hardly recognize her. First thing after breakfast I had her use a hair rinse. Kind of a mousy brown, but it'll wash right out."

"Fine," I said. "How's she holding up?"

There was a pause while Connie thought about it. "Pretty good, considering," she concluded. "Needs to stay close, but that doesn't bother me. In fact, I like it. I feel like a mother hen. Cluck cluck and all that. Also, there are certain things that Penny prefers not to discuss. Like anything that happened before yesterday. How about you?"

"Had an interesting discussion with her stepmother," I said, hesitating. "And a not-so-interesting talk with her father."

"And?"

"No conclusions, yet. Except one thing that really

bothers me. If Penny was your daughter and she ran away and you had a pretty good idea where she was going, wouldn't you follow her there? Drop everything and go get the kid back?"

"That would be a normal reaction, yes."

"Right," I said. "Makes you think, don't it? Jake and Lee Ann seem to be lacking in certain normal reactions. I get the distinct impression they're going through the motions, that they're not really all that eager to have her back home. Does that mean they're hiding something? Beats me. I've got an appointment later this afternoon with a *Miami Herald* reporter who may be able to shed a little light. Depending on what he has to say, I may or may not get back to the island tonight. Don't hold supper on my account."

Connie sighed. "Do what you have to do, T.D. Just be careful. What should I tell Penny?"

"Tell her I'm checking things out. Tell her she's safe."

Ah, safety. It was easy enough to say. But, as it happened, it was not something I was in a position to guarantee.

I lost my way, looking for Herald Plaza, and ended up in the city cemetery. That's not as bad as it sounds, though it did spook me some. In the light of afternoon the graveyard looked like a scale model for the future of the tropics, an island of discreet white condominium towers, entombed in concrete and frosted with stucco.

That was my mood when I finally entered the sleek *Miami Herald* building near the shores of Biscayne Bay. I practiced twiddling my thumbs while waiting for Stanley Horn, chief feature writer for the business section. There's more to thumb-twiddling than you might think. It takes skill and concentration. It takes panache.

Horn, who I'd never met, spotted me right off. I was a little surprised, since there were half a dozen others waiting in the reception area.

"You've got the raccoon look," he said.

"The what look?"

"Raccoon. You said you were a fishing guide, right? It's that pale circle around the eyes, from wearing polarized sunglasses. You wanted to talk about the Shake'n Jake Bonner thing, right? Buy me a coffee?"

"Surely," I said.

I followed Horn through a security checkpoint, down one floor, and into a staff cafeteria. We sat in the nonsmoking section because Horn, a round-shouldered man in his late forties, had asthma.

"What I should do is move to Arizona. Miami is no place for a bad set of air bags. Can't see it, somehow. I'd dry up and blow away, like a tumbleweed."

I said, "Tell me about Jake Bonner."

Horn made a steeple of his fingers and rested his chin on the point. He wore thick glasses that enlarged his watery brown eyes, making him look vulnerable. His confident tone of voice gave the opposite impression, however.

"Typical American success story, of a certain type. Came out of nowhere. Nowhere being Indigo Springs, a little cracker village in the Big Cypress. Jake was a big handsome kid from a big ugly family. Dirt poor. Marries a local rich girl against her parents' wishes. They run away to the big city, where Jake tends bar at a couple of local hotspots. Girl inherits money and Jake uses it to open a little nightclub. Five years later he's selling franchises. Barefoot boy makes million before he turns thirty. Sounds easy, huh?''

"You said Mary Beth inherited a few bucks."

"Mary Beth? Right, the wife. I tried to check that out and didn't get very far. Parents moved out of Indigo Springs after the daughter ran off. Settled in Marco Island, I think it was. Father made money in construction. He's the one who died. Drowned while tying up his boat, or something weird like that. Anyhow, Mary Beth inherited a hundred grand not long after they were married. Gave it to Jake and he got lucky and made a fortune with it."

"You think it was luck?"

He grinned and shook his head. He had tight, curly gray hair that fit him like a skullcap. "Not really. Some guys have the touch. For instance, if I decided to open up yet another Lauderdale nightspot, I'd be busted in six months. Not Jake Bonner. He's got the lucky touch. Now he's trying to promote yet another South Florida theme park. That means big bucks and big risk, but I wouldn't bet against him."

"He's got legal problems."

"So? Every mover and shaker has legal problems. Around here, in case you haven't noticed, they almost always get resolved in favor of the developer."

"You sound bitter."

He laughed. "What I am is green with envy. I write two features a week about people who are, from my point of view, fabulously wealthy. So it gets to me, just a little . . ." He paused and decided to come to the point. "You said something about a missing daughter. I checked that out with the Coral Gables cops. They have no such report."

He had me there. I hadn't thought to ask if the Bonners had talked to the local authorities. What they had done, as I informed Horn, was contact the Key West police. Who had in turn recommended me.

"You go after runaways, huh?"

"When the fish aren't biting," I said.

Horn stared at me, not quite sure he wanted to believe me. "Yeah, well, you must have plenty of business. This is the place people run to, from all over the country." He fiddled with the coffeecup, spinning it slowly in the saucer, as if it was a stage prop rather than something to drink from. "The daughter is what, eight years old? Seems a little young to leave home, even in this part of the world. I suppose you're going to tell me she's into drugs. Or prostitution."

"Nothing like that. Penny is still upset about her mother's death. Her running away has something to do with that."

When Horn laughed, the wheezing in his lungs became pronounced. He wasn't kidding about the asthma.

"I shouldn't," he said. "It's not funny. His wife gets hit by a car on their anniversary and five months later he marries the knock-'em-dead blonde who was driving the car. No wonder the little girl is confused."

"I was just wondering," I said, "why the *Herald* didn't do a story on the circumstances surrounding the death of Mary Beth Bonner."

Stanley Horn smiled. His magnified eyes were like brown fish in a pink aquarium. "I get it," he said.

"You want to know if there's a cover-up. Local business mogul bumps off wife, local media suppresses the awful truth. Like that?"

"Or any variation thereof."

"I guess you don't know much about the way the *Herald* operates, Mr. Stash."

"Just Stash, or T.D. Mister makes me nervous. You're right about me not knowing how the paper operates," I said. "I'm hoping you'll tell me."

"Deal," he said. "First, my editor would *love* a nice scandalous murder. Bastard would probably give it to one of the crime reporters, though. If it's business-related, I'd get to do a few sidebars, maybe a personality piece. That's the way it works on a publication the size of this. Matter of fact, the blood-and-guts boys checked in with me right after the accident. This is way before Jake married what's-her-name, the blonde with the sexy voice."

"Lee Ann. She was a disc jockey."

"Yeah, right. Some little station in Lauderdale beach, wasn't it? Now Bonner is talking about making her communications director when Gator World opens. She's done pretty well by herself, you ask me."

I said, "So you think it was a setup?"

He grinned. "That was my first conclusion, until I checked out Bonner's finances. In the business world, typically the motivation for spouse-killing is insurance or inheritance. Well, the first wife had already inherited, so I checked out the insurance angle. As it happened, Bonner didn't have a big policy on his wife. It was like twenty-five grand, which is about what he clears from the Shake'n Jake franchises in one week. Wouldn't buy coffee for the construction crew, he ever gets Gator World really rolling. So as a

61

motive, insurance is out. This I got from the claims adjuster. He's the one did all the legwork. Checked out Jake, his wife, and the future Mrs. Jake. Told me the marriage was solid. The accident was just what it looked like. An accident."

"Can you give me his name, the claims adjuster?"

Horn shrugged. "Why not? Only if he's found anything interesting, tell him to get back to me. If it turns out Mr. Gator World really is a wife-killer, I want at least a shot at the story." He wrote down the adjuster's name and told me he could be found in the Pompano Beach phone book. "Let me ask you something," he said, handing me the scrap of paper. "Who are you really working for?"

"Bonner has agreed to pay me if I locate his daughter," I said. "The way I prefer to think of it, though, is I'm working for the little girl, Penny."

The fish eyes blinked. It was like watching a light flashing on and off. "You're serious," he said, sounding surprised.

"Very," I said. "A certain party says the little girl ran away because she's afraid of her father. Penny thinks Jake and Lee Ann conspired to murder her mother."

"A certain party, huh? Who told you that?"

"I'm not at liberty to say."

"Buddy boy, you sound like a rookie reporter. It was the girl told you that, right? You've found the girl and now you're holding out on Jake Bonner."

"You've got it wrong. I haven't got the girl. Not yet."

The trick with telling a convincing fib is, you can't look away. Drop your eyes and your goose is cooked. Stanley Horn knew the trick, too, and he waited. Although I didn't blink, he remained unconvinced.

"Something's off," he said. "I can smell it."

"Must be the cream in your coffee."

"Tell me this. Is the little girl okay?"

I said, "That's what I heard."

Horn grinned. Then he thanked me for the coffee he didn't drink, and showed me to the door.

Must be the crazies in your minds.

What time is the little red clock.

Born twisted. Then he reached me for the corner he didn't drink, not throwing it to th

8

I drove up to Pompano Beach and sat in a bar overlooking a marina basin. I nursed a bottle of Ballantine India Pale Ale and watched the sailboats backing up in the canal, waiting for the bridge to open. A whining pop song spewed from the jukebox. Every twenty minutes or so I'd peel a quarter off the counter and go to the pay phone and ring Bert Hamper's number.

Bert Hamper was the insurance adjuster who handled the claim on Mary Beth. The interesting thing about Bert was that he didn't answer his phone, nor did he have an answering machine do it for him. Probably the only insurance man in South Florida who wasn't intravenously connected to his telephone.

It got to be a game, going to the pay phone. After about the fifth try the brawny kid tending bar asked me if I was a dope dealer. He wasn't kidding.

"Not that I care," he said. "Only if that's what you're doing, take it elsewhere."

"You sound like you've been burned," I said.

He shrugged in a way that showed off his biceps, letting me know how tough he was. Jug-handle ears added to the effect. "We had a problem last week," he said. "Asshole was sitting right where you're sitting. All the time back and forth to the pay phone. Turns out he fished a bale out of the bay, and he's got it in the cockpit of his Boston whaler, parked right down there in the canal tied up to the marina dock. What he's doing on the phone is lining up a buyer."

"What happened?"

"One of the people he called was an undercover cop," the bartender said, flexing his crew cut. "They busted him, right where you're sitting."

I moved over one seat. "I wouldn't know what a bale of marijuana looks like," I said.

"Yeah, sure."

"I've been trying to call my wife. She ran off with Barry Manilow."

"Give me a break, pal."

"I tied a yellow ribbon around the old ficus tree, but she forgot all about me."

"Finish the beer and beat it. You give me a headache."

"That's what my wife said."

Bars aren't as friendly as they used to be in Pompano Beach. I left Jughead the sticky quarter as a tip and drove to Bert Hamper's address, intending to slip a note under the door if all else failed.

Thinking back on it, I'm almost sure there was a black El Camino pickup in the parking lot when I left the bar. It didn't register at the time. And if I happened to notice it tailing me over to Hamper's place, I didn't give it a second thought. There are a lot of El Caminos in the world, and I had no reason to think I was being followed.

That's what I tell myself when I wake up with the sweats. The truth is that I had unwittingly intruded myself into a situation over which I had no control. Hard as I tried.

I found the Bert Hamper residence. It was a small

bungalow on a backwater canal. Cinder block with a tin roof. Not so very different from my house, come to think. Except for the new fifty-two-foot ketch parked in the canal behind the house. The aluminum masts towered over the little bungalow. There was an old Cadillac under the carport. Newer than my coupe, but still old by Pompano Beach standards.

The door buzzer produced a brassy exclamation, *ta da*! If you pressed quick enough, it almost came to crescendo. I imagined a manic orchestra conductor responding in pantomine. After I got bored with playing doorbell games, I went out back and had to resist the impulse to genuflect to the awesome ketch. It overwhelmed the modest neighborhood.

I looked at the gold-leafed name on the fat transom and winced.

"Ahoy the *My Way*! Anybody home? Bert?"

The ketch was serene in its silence. The water in the canal was the color of rust, and mirror-still.

"Over here, young man."

The voice was reedy, feminine, and old. I had trouble locating the source.

"Over here," the old woman said. "I'm the good neighbor."

She was sitting under the fringe of a large shade umbrella in the yard next door. The ground around her was hard-baked. Gravel showed through the few remaining tufts of bermuda grass. Nearby a limp-fronded Christmas palm was slowly giving up the ghost. Paradise neglected, unraveling into a small patch of desert.

The old woman in the ruined garden was Eileen Murphy, a widow, and she knew all about Bert Hamper.

"Sit down, young man," she said after inviting me

66

over. "It makes me tired the way everyone stands, or walks, or runs. And if you're looking for Bert, you'll want to sit down."

I sat.

Mrs. Murphy screwed a low-tar cigarette into a long, enameled holder. "When you get to be my age you're allowed an affectation. This is my Bette Davis butt-holder. Keeps my knuckles from going yellow." She held the contraption fairly steady while I persuaded a heavy brass table lighter to ignite. "Thanks. You want the truth, I suppose?"

"Yes," I said, a little taken aback.

Mrs. Murphy smiled. Her flesh pleated and puckered, but the effect was not displeasing. "The truth is I use the holder because the nerves in my hands are bad. I can't feel the cigarette when it burns down. Are you a friend of Bert's? Business acquaintance?"

"A little of each, I guess. When my car got stolen, Bert checked out the claim. He was very helpful."

"Mmmm," the old woman said, sucking at the stem of the holder. Her eyes were bright and amused.

"We got to talking boats," I said, eyeing the big ketch. "The sneak never told me he had a new Irwin. It's a real beauty."

"Mmmmm. Lovely."

"I've been calling Bert all afternoon, Mrs. Murphy. Do you know where I can find him, by any chance? I've got some business I can throw his way."

"The poor man's in Pittsburgh," she said. "Buried there," she added, waiting happily for my reaction.

"Bert *died*, Mrs. Murphy? When did it happen?"

"Fourth of July weekend. The poor man had the yacht delivered just the week before. Like a little boy, he was. 'I'm heading for the blue horizon,' he told me, 'sailing the seven seas.' Oh, he was enthralled with the idea. It breaks my heart to think they buried him in Pittsburgh. He so wanted to go to the Bahamas. 'I'll get this tub to Freeport if it kills me.' I don't know how many times I heard him say that. That's the saddest part, that he never got there."

"Is that where he died, Mrs. Murphy, Pittsburgh?"

"Gracious, no! He died right here." She pointed the cigarette holder at the ketch. "There's no more than five feet of water in that canal, so they tell me, but it was enough to drown Bert. I keep thinking that if he'd only just stood up, he'd be alive today. He was a tall man. As tall as you. If you fell in shallow water, you'd just stand up, wouldn't you?"

"I'd try, Mrs. Murphy. How did it happen?"

The light was beginning to fade. The canal water had turned as black as marble. The glowing ember of the old woman's cigarette wobbled like a firefly.

"I was up quite late, for me. If I sit right here, I can see the fireworks at the beach, in that patch of sky over there. Bert was working on his new boat. Doing I don't know what all. Just playing on it, I suppose. He was retiring, did you know that?"

"No," I said. "I had no idea."

The old woman smiled, squinting her eyes. "Well, I think it was a little bit of a secret. He won all that money and he decided to buy the boat and just sail away. You *did* know he gambled?"

I chuckled and shook my head. "I guess I didn't know Bert very well, Mrs. Murphy. All we ever talked about was sailboats."

"Well, he liked the ponies, Bert Hamper did. Used to sit right out there by the canal and study the racing form. This was before he had the boat, of course. He was a smart, careful man, but I don't think he ever won very much until he hit the—what is it called, the triple thing?"

"The Trifecta?"

"That's it! Made me promise not to breathe a word. I think he was going to cheat on the tax," Mrs. Murphy whispered, delighted with the idea. "And how would the tax people find him, if he was sailing the seven seas? Except the poor man got all tangled up in that rope and drowned."

"Rope?"

"From the boat. I suppose he'd had a few cocktails. Why not? It was a holiday. I had a drink or two myself, before going in. He was nice enough to turn the music up for me. Frank Sinatra. I love Sinatra, and so did Bert. That's what we had in common. You saw the name of the boat?"

"*My Way.*"

Mrs. Murphy hummed a few bars. "He'd put a record player on the boat, and he turned it up so I could hear. Always the gentleman. I told his daughter I was *quite* sure he didn't want to be buried in Pittsburgh, but she told me to mind my own business."

"I don't understand about the rope, Mrs. Murphy."

"They say he must have been coiling it up when he slipped and fell over the side. He was all tangled up in it when they pulled him out of the water. The coroner said it was mis-adventure. I didn't understand that at all. He'd never got to go on his adventure. It doesn't seem fair, does it?"

"No," I said. "It doesn't."

9

I left Pompano Beach feeling mighty pleased with myself. I'd managed to fool an old widow into telling me that Bert Hamper had come into a large sum of money and then died under circumstances that were, at the least, highly suspicious.

What that did was put a new twist on my thinking. The chain of coincidence had a weak link. Hamper's story about keeping his big track win a secret so he could cheat the tax man was a convenient fiction to placate a nosy neighbor. As every gambler knows, when a substantial sum is involved, the IRS gets its cut before the track pays out. I suspected that old "My Way" Bert had won his prize money elsewhere, that his good fortune—temporary, as it turned out—was the result of an investigation into a related piece of misadventure. The accidental death of Mary Beth Bonner.

Murder and blackmail. The old one-two combination. It didn't really matter whose idea the murder was. Jake or Lee Ann, take your pick. As for motive, it might have been as simple and deadly as passion. Maybe Jake had tired of his wife and wanted to trade up to the new model. Divorce, in his highly leveraged situation, would have been ruinous. As his business partner, Mary Beth would have been entitled to at least half the fortune they had accumulated. See you later, Gator World.

That was the murder part, according to my new theory. The blackmail, if the premise held, had been the brainchild of Bert Hamper. In the course of a routine death-benefit investigation he'd uncovered something damaging about Jake and Lee Ann and used it to buy an early retirement aboard a luxury sailboat. The Sinatra fan had done it his way, and retirement had come even more suddenly than expected.

Of course, I had not one shred of evidence. Not even enough to interest the average grand jury. All of my clever surmises were based on the testimony of a frightened, resentful child. Nevertheless, I did not really believe that Penny was in danger. I was willing to accept the premise, in theory, that Lee Ann had intentionally run down Mary Beth and that the couple had later conspired to silence an extortionist, but I just didn't buy the idea that Jake Bonner intended to have his nine-year-old daughter killed.

It went against nature. Husband kills wife . . . yes. Wife kills husband . . . sure. Father cold-bloodedly plots murder of his only child . . . hardly ever. Deliberate infanticide was the act of a psychopath, and Jake Bonner wasn't a psychopath. He was self-centered and obsessed with success, but not so fundamentally damaged that he would want to turn out the lights in those innocent green eyes.

No way.

That's what I surmised, in my self-satisfied way. Too content with my cleverness to check in the rearview mirror for the El Camino pickup with the tinted windows. I had fooled the old widow and I had fooled Jake Bonner. I was so damned cute no one would think to put a tail on me.

The ancient Greeks called it hubris and wrote tragedies about it. In the keys we call it dumb stupidity, and have another rum.

The tail was there, had been all the way from Gator World, but it just didn't register. When I pulled into the big parking area surrounding the Key Largo Shake'n Jake's, I never even thought to look behind me.

The club was much as Lil Cashman had described it. Neon flamingos, potted palms, smoke and mirrors. The sound was stunning. I could feel my ribs vibrating before I'd gotten through the foyer. The bar was shaped like an S and padded in hot-pink Naugahyde. The young ladies behind the bar wore matching pink tights and little silk jockey-style shirts, and that was about it. The drinks came out of automatic dispensers, so the barmaids could concentrate on looking good and moving to the incessant music.

I drank my glass thimble of rum and looked around. The joint was jumping. Dancers writhed on every square foot of the big, multilevel dance floor. The illusion of space was doubled and redoubled in the mirrored walls and ceiling. Counting heads would take a lot of concentration. Not that I was in a counting mood. I was more than willing to let the accountants do that. If they looked hard enough, there was a pretty good chance they would find, missing from the books, the price of an Irwin 52, loaded.

That was going to be my next gambit. Find a way to audit Jake Bonner. Nail him on points. If Bert Hamper did it, so could I. It was a nice plan, simple and clean. What to do about Penny was not so clear.

Maybe Connie would have some ideas. And there was always the grandmother, up there in Marco Island.

I took my time over the second automatically dispensed rumlike drink and let the Pointer Sisters rattle my skull for a while. Never talked to anyone inside the club. My grasp of sign language is sadly lacking. When I was good and ready, I segued into the parking lot and drove on home.

There was nothing unusual about the headlights that followed behind me. Just headlights. You expect to have headlights behind you on the Overseas Highway. It's a very busy road. In the keys it's the *only* road.

I led them to her, of course. I went directly to Connie's house. It was ten o'clock and I was tired and road-weary, but I wanted to check on my girls.

Penny answered the door. She was wearing a new pair of pajamas. Like a damn fool I let her stand there in the light coming from inside so I could admire the new pajamas. They had cute little rabbits all over them.

Hippety-hop.

"Hello, stranger," Connie said, holding open the screen and scooting us both inside, out of the light. She paused in the doorway for a moment, looking out at the dark street. Then she closed the door and turned to me and said, "You smell like you've been drinking cheap perfume."

I didn't intend to stay long. Just long enough to assure Penny that her beautiful stepmother hadn't put a spell on me and that I had no intention of turning her in. The subject of what would happen to Penny if I succeeded in proving her allegations was so vast and scary it did not seem appropriate to discuss it at night, before bed. I did ask about her maternal grandmother.

Penny's response was guarded. "I talked to her once," she said. "Last year on my birthday. I wasn't supposed to, but I did."

"Your mother and father didn't want you communicating with your grandmother? Why?"

"Dad said she was sick in the head and it was like an infection and I'd get it. I didn't think you could get infections over the phone, so when Gramma called, I listened. All she said was she wanted me to have a happy birthday. Mom and Dad were real upset when they found out."

"Have you met your grandmother?"

"When I was a little baby, I guess. I don't remember. She and my mom had a big fight when my grandfather died. I don't remember that, either, except sometimes my mom and dad would talk about it when they didn't think I was listening. Dad would talk about how Gramma was crazy and my mother shouldn't believe anything she said."

It was just one big, happy family. The green money snake had gotten into the garden and spoiled the picnic. Reptiles will do that, especially the human kind. I thought, fleetingly, of the Cullen brothers, and then pushed them from my mind. The hour was too late for boogeymen. I wanted to get home and brush the taste of cheap rum from my mouth.

"Penny, we're going to have to take this one day at a time, okay? Right now the only promise I can make is that you're safe here."

I think she really and truly believed me. When the child had been put to bed, Connie took me aside.

She wanted to be reassured that Penny was in no immediate danger of being returned to her father.

"We've got no legal right to keep her from him," I said. "You know that."

"Never mind legal," Connie said. "Somebody has frightened that child half to death. Was it the stepmother?"

I shrugged and dropped onto the divan. Connie settled next to me, resting a hand on my knee. She smelled faintly of fresh clay. It was a cool, comforting scent.

"I don't know about Lee Ann," I said. "She's not your typical wicked-stepmother archetype, that's for sure. She sounded pretty convincing in her concern for Penny. But there's something out of focus about Jake Bonner. I got the distinct impression he was more interested in his current project than the fact that his only child has run away. He acts like it's an inconvenience. He seems to have no idea why Penny might have problems adjusting to the fact that he married the woman responsible for her mother's death. That's a hell of a lot to expect from a nine-year-old."

"Bullheaded fathers aren't exactly an endangered species," Connie said. "Especially where daughters are concerned."

I nodded. "If it was just stubbornness, something could be worked out. I think Jake Bonner's too smart to be just plain pigheaded. I think he's afraid of Penny. Afraid of what she knows."

"Any ideas?"

"Maybe it's exactly what Penny has been telling us. That her mother's death was no accident. Lee Ann and Jake claim they didn't know each other before Mary Beth was killed, that the tragedy brought them together. They *had* to say that. But what if Penny knows better? At this point I'm inclined to believe her. Lee Ann tells a cute story, but it starts to go sour when you tack on an insurance investigator who got rich quick and then drowned on the very day Lee Ann Chambers became the second Mrs. Bonner. The whole setup is just too damned convenient."

"What are you going to do about it?"

I yawned and glanced at my watch. "Dunno exactly. Put enough together to turn it over to the cops, I guess. If I can prove Jake and Lee Ann knew each other prior to Mary Beth's death, that ought to be enough to initiate a homicide investigation. With a legal basis to proceed, the police can subpoena Bonner's books. They may not be able to prove that Mary Beth's death was intentional, but if they can establish that Jake paid off the insurance investigator, they may be able to stick him with that murder. It's going to be tough, though. He's got the dough to buy lots of protection, legal and otherwise."

Connie said, "And what will happen to Penny?"

"I wish I knew. A foster home, a relative, maybe. There's Grandmother up in Marco Island. For now, I'm going to do exactly what I told the kid to do. Take it one day at a time."

Connie embraced me at the door. It was more than a friendly hug.

"You can stay the night," she said. "In my bed or elsewhere, your choice."

"I better go home, Con. I'm beat. Rain check?"

"Nope," she said with a lopsided grin. "One-time offer. No returns or exchanges."

"I still better go home."

Her shrug was worth a thousand words. Bemusement, regret, and relief being only three of them. She smiled and said, "One other thing, T.D. I want to keep her."

"What?"

"I'm serious. I want to keep Penny and help her grow up, and do the best I can to make things right. Sound crazy?"

"Not at all."

"I know it's impossible, legally. Single foster parent and all that. I just wanted you to know how I feel about it. Now you do."

"Now I do," I said.

I kissed her good-bye.

10

THE sirens woke me. I tried to stay down under,
several fathoms into a dream. Couldn't hold it. Another big one that got away. The sirens were confused, approaching from several directions. Boxing
the compass with an annoying *wee-waa, wee-waa*.

Fire engines. Police cars. An ambulance.

I was in my own bed, safe between clean sheets,
content to remain horizontal. It was five o'clock, the
hour before dawn. The sirens meant trouble for someone else, not me.

Wrong again.

The sun was rising much too soon, turning the
window blinds bright orange. I got out of bed and
popped the blinds, and suddenly I was wide awake.

The sky was on fire.

It didn't really hit home until I'd dressed and
walked to the corner and saw the flames sky-jumping
on Eaton Street. Then my brain put together fire,
Eaton Street, and Connie Geiger's place, and I must
have run all the way because I was out of breath and
bathed in sweat when a volunteer fireman tackled
me a few yards shy of what had been Connie's front
door.

"Are you nuts?" he said, dragging me back out of
the blazing heat. "Are you out of your mind?"

I guess maybe I was, just a little. The fire made me crazy. It made the inside of my head itch.

"That's a gas fire," someone said. "It's like a blast furnace in there."

Later it was determined that the fire had started with a minor explosion from the kiln and that flames fed by the ruptured propane tank had engulfed the studio and adjacent house in a matter of moments.

I didn't know that then. I only knew that no one, not the firemen or the cops or the neighbors, seemed to know the whereabouts of Connie Geiger and her young guest.

It was Detective Lieutenant Nelson Kerry who finally convinced me to sit down on the curb and drink a cup of coffee. Behind us jets of water and damping chemicals vanished into the flames. The old, wooden frame structure began to crumble, folding into the heat.

"Let me get this straight," the lieutenant said, crouching next to me. "You have reason to believe Miss Geiger is inside the residence. You think there's another person in there with her. Is that right?"

"The son of a bitch," I said. "He must have had me followed. He *must* have."

"First, tell me about Miss Geiger and her house-guest."

The jive I'd given to the Detective Sergeant Sawyer was only slightly exaggerated. Nel Kerry and I go way back, to the time in grade school when having a best friend was just about the most important thing in the world. More important than baseball or comic books or candy bars. That faded over the years, like it almost always does, and in its place a new wariness developed when Nel became a cop and I became an unlicensed troublemaker. What

79

makes Nel Kerry uneasy is the notion that one day he will have to arrest me.

We both have a working relationship with the law, but he is on the inside and I am on the outside, and that was never more apparent than when I told him the truth about Penny Bonner. I told him about Jake and Lee Ann and the peculiar circumstance of their marriage, and the even more peculiar coincidence involving the late Bert Hamper, insurance investigator. Then I told him how I had decided to take responsibility for Penny myself, because the child had believed her life to be in danger. Quite correctly, as it turned out. The truth of it was burning behind us.

"You *what?*" Nel said finally, with a tone of disbelief.

"I left her with Connie. It seemed like a reasonable thing to do. She was scared of her father."

"You're telling me this is the kid on the poster, right? The one whose father called me to report her missing, and I told him to call you. Correct?"

"I screwed up, Nel," I said, staring at the flames. The substance of the house was almost consumed and the fire was beginning to burn itself out. "I didn't think he'd kill her. It was either Jake or one of his henchmen who torched the place. Had to be. Nel, you've got to put out an APB on a black El Camino. Late model, tinted windows."

"I don't know about that," he said. "I do agree with one thing, though. You screwed everything up, T.D. This time you surely did. Now, come on over here, I want to show you something."

I followed him to his cruiser, parked in the street with the lights flashing. He unlocked the right rear door and opened it.

"Penny!"

She was shivering, soaking wet, wrapped in a blanket, hugging her backpack.

"Looks like what happened, your friend Miss Geiger grabbed the girl and shoved her down into an old rainwater cistern that runs under the kitchen. She was able to crawl out that way. Miss Geiger wasn't so lucky."

When I reached out to touch her, Penny hid herself under the blanket and cried, "I'm sorry I'm sorry I'm sorry."

Nel took me aside. "She'll be okay. Physically, anyhow. I tried talking to her; she wouldn't even tell me her name. Just keeps apologizing. Which makes me think maybe she was the one started the fire. Playing with matches is not exactly unusual behavior for an emotionally disturbed child. Hell, T.D., I'm not saying it was intentional. The girl probably believes all those lies she's told you."

"You're out of your mind, Nel. You're flat dead wrong."

He stared at me and said, "Maybe. Maybe not. But I'm going to hold her for now and notify her parents, and then we'll see. And what you're going to do is go home and change your clothes and calm yourself down. Then call up Lil Cashman and the both of you come down to my office and explain to me, very carefully, why you shouldn't be arrested and charged with harboring a fugitive minor."

"That's how you see it?"

"That's how I see it."

I went to the car. Penny remained under the blanket, shivering, hiding her head. I said, "Penny, I know that none of this is your fault. Not the fire, not Connie, not anything."

Penny wouldn't come out from under the blanket. She wanted to hide there. I didn't blame her.

Nel pulled me away from the car and locked the door, leaning against the cruiser with his arms folded. "Your active involvement in this matter is over. Now go on home, call Lil Cashman like I said. We'll discuss this in my office."

As I left, the ambulance crew was taking something from the smoldering wreckage of the house. I looked away. I didn't want to see what they were zipping into the long black bag.

The little green lizard came out of the crack in the tiles and stood under the shower with me, a few inches from my feet. Probably the water had stunned him, but I took it as confirmation that life itself was seriously out of kilter. Connie's death had blurred reality. It wouldn't have surprised me to see dogs walking on their hind legs down Duval Street, or toads flying through the air. The rough beast had slouched into Old Town, loosing a nightmare anarchy, and nothing would ever be the same again.

That insanity was thick upon us had been affirmed by Nel Kerry's willingness to blame Penny for the fire. He thought I was around the bend with my theory about Jake and Lee Ann. From his by-the-book perspective I'd started to get out of line the moment I decided not to turn Penny over to the relevant authorities. Now he was going to correct my initial mistake.

Water and soap and shampoo erased the stink of the fire from my skin and hair. I could still smell it, though, deep inside. I threw the clothes I had been wearing in the trash and went to the closet. Unlike Jake Bonner I didn't have a white linen power suit.

The best I could do was a seersucker job that went with a pair of scuffed white bucks and a necktie that had been in fashion when *The Waltons* was prime-time. I had to think about how to knot the tie—that's how long it had been. When the noose was on, I went to the mirror and slicked back my hair, striving for an effect that made me look less like a fishing guide and more like somebody's father.

The costume made me feel slightly ridiculous. Considering my state of mind, that was an improvement. My little subterfuge, conceived under the shower, would either work or not. I had to give it a shot, although there seemed little chance of pulling it off. I'd been out of step with Jake Bonner from the beginning. The momentum was in his favor.

A change of clothes went into a duffel bag. Ditto for a pair of sneaks, a shaving kit, and the .38 Smith & Wesson revolver Nel Kerry had sold me, once upon a time. I added a box of cartridges, thought about Ellis and Orrin Cullen, the Swamp Thing twins, and retrieved a Ruger M-77 deer rifle from the cupboard where I store my fishing gear and other assorted items. The Ruger wouldn't fit in the duffel bag, so I wrapped it in a towel and put it in the trunk of the coupe, along with the machete I keep on hand in case I ever get the urge to cut sugarcane for Castro.

The last thing I did before leaving the house was call Lily Cashman. She was in bed, awaiting a breakfast prepared by Sami.

"Stash, honey," she purred, "can you be a doll and ring me later, at the office? Sam is trying out our new crepe pan."

"Won't take a minute, Lil. Just wanted to warn you that Nel Kerry is going to want to talk to you about me, regarding the Penny Bonner thing. I want you to tell him the truth, so far as you know it. He'll make a lot of threatening noises, but you'll be okay."

"What's going on?"

"I'm in trouble, Lil, and I'm going to get in a lot more of it very soon."

"Hang on. I'm on my way over. Don't do anything until—"

"Don't bother," I said. "I'm already gone."

First stop was a car-rental outfit on Roosevelt Boulevard. I had to wait for the Conch Train, which was running its first load of tourists around the island. When the train was clear, I pulled the coupe into the lot, put up the convertible top, and used plastic to lease a generic-looking sedan. Then I transferred the duffel bag and the Ruger and the machete into the new-smelling trunk and drove around to Mutt Durgin's bait shack.

Mutt didn't recognize me in the seersucker suit. He brushed donut crumbs from his T-shirt, placed his coffeecup on the crab trap that serves as his table, and stood up, ready to be of service to a potential customer.

"Relax," I said, lifting my shades. "You're not getting any money out of me. Matter of fact, I'm here to beg some from you."

"T.D.? Shee-it, man, I never see'd you in a monkey suit. And damn, you all combed up and groomed. Let me guess, you're on your way to court, right?"

"Eventually, no doubt. I intend to delay the appearance for a while. What have you got for spare-type cash?"

Mutt listened to a rundown of what had happened and a rough outline of what I planned to do about it. Bless him, he went directly to the cash box and insisted I take it all.

"You call me when you get where you're goin'. I can wire more. Money ain't no problem. You sure you don't want me ridin' shotgun?"

It was better that Mutt remain at the dock, tending to business, and I said so.

"Have it your way," he said. "Only remember you just gotta gimme a shout and I'll come running. Hold on, bubba," he added as I turned to leave. "Just a minute here, I gotta goin'-away present."

He rummaged behind the counter and emerged with a Ka-bar knife in a leather leg sheath.

"Bought this drunk," he said. "Never had no use for it. Maybe you will."

I hefted the knife. It was a solid item, of the type favored by jarheads and gator-skinners. Not my kind of weapon, but I wasn't in a position to decline any contributions to the small armory I'd stashed in the trunk of the rental car.

"Never mind about no dumb-ass heroics," he advised. "Just you be ready to duck."

"Later, Mutt. And much obliged."

I pulled over near a pay phone, a block or so from the Key West Police Station. While the phone was ringing, I held my breath so that when Nel Kerry answered my voice was convincingly harried.

"Got the Cullen brothers, Nel," I panted. "Holed up at the Sea View, on South Street. I'm going in."

I hung up and counted. Nel Kerry was a good man. Out the door and into his unmarked car before I got to twenty. Followed by a bunch of uniforms who tumbled into cruisers and followed his screeching tires. I gave it ten more and pulled the rental car around to Angela Street and went in the side entrance.

"Sir?"

I didn't know the man at the desk and he didn't know me. That was my first piece of luck.

"Jake Bonner," I said, pumping his hand. "You all got my little girl here somewheres."

The desk man tried to put me off until the lieutenant returned. I was a powerful businessman, used to having my way, and wouldn't hear of it.

"Just let me see her with my own eyes," I said. "Make sure you all didn't screw up, find the wrong girl."

Penny was in the interrogation room, adjacent to Nel's empty office. A young, light-skinned black woman was trying to persuade her to eat a fast-food breakfast from a Styrofoam container. Penny was clutching her blue backpack to her chest and rocking, not looking at the matron or the food.

"Penny," I cried, letting my voice break. "Come here and give your dad a great big hug."

Penny's instincts were right on. She looked at me and did not speak. I scooped her up in my arms and made a shushing sound in her ear. She responded by tucking her head under my chin and holding on tight, locking her legs around my waist.

"Oh, honey, your mom and I been scared crazy," I said, rocking her. "Everything's gonna be okay now, everything's fine."

I smiled at the matron, who wasn't sure how to react. Whatever instructions Nel Kerry had given her didn't involve dealing with Jake Bonner. To her credit the matron seemed happy to be witnessing a father-and-daughter reunion.

"The lieutenant be back soon," she said. "He wants to confer with you, regarding the, ah, situation."

"Sure thing," I said. "Anything the man wants.

Come on, honey," I said to Penny, "know what your dad left out at the desk? Your extra-special birthday doll."

The matron threw up her hands and smiled, surrendering to parental imperative.

I carried Penny out past the desk and went on out of the building and became, just like that, a wanted man.

11

IT was a smooth deal until we hit a traffic jam on Big Pine Key, thirty miles out of Key West. It doesn't take much to back up traffic on the Overseas Highway. A minor accident, a breakdown on one of the bridges, even a flat tire will do, if the flow is heavy.

Penny was crouched on the floor in front of the passenger seat. Most of the brown tint had washed out of her hair and the copper-red shone through the tangles. The sky-blue backpack was under her, not so much for comfort as security. It was a lucky piece, having come through the fire and the police station.

The first thing she'd wanted to know, as we made good our escape from the police station, was what had happened to Connie Geiger.

"They wouldn't tell me, so I figured she was dead. Is she?"

My initial impulse was to soften the blow with a well-intentioned falsehood. Something along the lines of Connie being in the hospital. The green eyes bored into me, though, and I found myself speaking the truth. Telling her that Connie had died in the fire.

Penny dropped her chin and stared at her knees as we sped along, putting miles between us and Key

West. The child seemed to be beyond tears. Her voice was small and tight, as if something had her by the throat. They had been awakened just before dawn, she said, by a banging noise. Like a hammer hitting metal. A hollow sound.

"Connie said it was someone fooling around near the kiln. She told me to get dressed and then she went out to the living room to call you up. Only right away there was a boom and the whole house shook and then everything was burning. Connie shoved me down into the wet place under the kitchen floor. There was just room enough for me and my backpack. That's when I figured it all out, while I was hiding in there."

"What was that?" I asked. "What did you figure out?"

Penny sounded bitter beyond her years. "They came to get me, only instead they got Connie. They killed her, just like they killed my mom. They'll kill you, too. Everyone who helps will get killed. Because of me."

I tried to reassure her. It was far from an easy task, especially when my concentration was broken by the necessity of checking the rearview mirror for cop cars or El Camino pickups or metallic-red Porsches.

"Penny," I said, "the best thing for you would be if you could stay in a safe place with someone you trust and talk about all the bad things that have happened to you. That would make you feel better."

"I doubt it," she said darkly.

"What I was going to say, unfortunately we can't do that right this minute. We've got to get you away from your father."

She nodded vigorously. "And Lee Ann."

"Yes. What I have in mind, we drive on up to

Marco Island and see if we can find your grandmother. Would you like to see her?"

I couldn't tell if her tentative nod signified lack of enthusiasm or fear that we'd never get there. I didn't push it. It was enough that we have a destination. As destinations go, a grandmother's house was as good as any. I thought of it as a potential sanctuary, a place where Penny could be left in safe hands, allowing me the freedom of movement to neutralize Jake Bonner, if only I could find a way.

How that little task was to be accomplished was still very much up in the air. Hunches and theories would not convince a just-the-facts lawman like Nel Kerry. I had to get the goods on Bonner. I had to prove that he was the criminal, not me.

"How come we're stopped?" Penny asked uneasily. "Traffic's backed up."

It was the north lane that was jammed. The southbound lane was moving along at a fair pace. I leaned out the window with the biggest good-old-boy grin I could muster and flagged a passing Volvo, on the theory that Swedes are friendly.

"Hey, buddy, what's the problem up there?" I said. "Accident?"

The driver of the Volvo had a flaking, sunburned face and a Chaplin-type mustache. He didn't mind telling me what was going on, not a bit. It was typical keys nonsense, he said. A roadblock.

"They got three carloads of county sheriffs. They got the highway patrol. They got some dude looks like Wyatt Earp, with pearl-handled revolvers. Stopping every northbound vehicle. They check the driver's license, ask a few questions, and the Wyatt Earp guy checks the inside of the car. That's it."

"Oh, yeah?" I said. Trying to sound merely interested.

"I mean, do they really think random checks are going to slow down the drug-runners?" The driver shook his head, amused at the stupidity of the local authorities. "All they're doing is screwing up traffic, giving everybody bad vibes, you know what I mean?"

"Sure do," I said, and waved. Thank you, Mr. Motorist.

The Wyatt Earp with the pearl-handled revolvers would be Tyrone Whiddon, a Monroe County sheriff. Who knew me by sight. I'd expected Nel Kerry to react quickly, but had hoped it wouldn't come to something as drastic and unpopular as a Lower Keys roadblock. No such luck. Proceed to Plan B.

"A slight change of plans," I explained to Penny. "I think what we'll do is go fishing."

I wheeled the rental car out of the northbound lane—just another pissed-off motorist—and retreated south to Cudjoe Key.

"Are they after us?" Penny asked. She hunched herself farther under the dash.

"We're just going to be careful, that's all. Assuming you have no objection to a boat ride."

Penny shrugged. I got the idea that if I'd suggested jumping out of an aircraft *sans* parachute, her reaction would have been the same. The child had been introduced to fatalism as a way of life. That was a damn shame. It made me want to kick Jake Bonner in the shins, just for starters.

There was a new marina on the Gulf side of Cudjoe Key. It was marked by a sign on the highway, directing customers to an unpaved road. After taking the turn, I pulled the car over and got out with the duffel bag. Using a stand of mangroves as cover, I shed the seersucker suit and the white bucks and the tie and emerged in khakis, workshirt, and sneakers. I tried uncombing my hair and decided the wind would do it for me soon enough.

The staff at the Angler's Paradise Marina couldn't have been more helpful. They fixed me up with an eighteen-foot fiberglass bass boat equipped with a fifty-horse outboard and a spray dodger. I rented two spin-casting rods to make it look good and then laid it on thick by asking what lures might attract the red snapper and cobia my daughter and I hoped to catch. I bought the recommended lures and a chart of the local "secret" hot spots. A glance at Penny's freckles reminded me to get her a visor and sunscreen. We then bought packaged sandwiches, as many as could be purchased without attracting attention, and a small Styrofoam cooler to hold ice and water.

I paid for the whole mess with plastic. They took the imprint of the charge card and left the total open, which was just as well, considering what I had in mind for the boat. As a show of faith, I left the keys to the rental car, "just in case you have to move it."

"We like to have all the boats back at the dock by five-thirty," the young lady at the register informed me. "That way the boys can make sure they're cleaned up and they can top off the gas and stuff."

"Sure thing," I said. "Pam'll be ready for supper by then, won't you, Pam?"

"Yes, Dad," Penny said.

"I think we'll try our luck at Bow Channel first," I said.

"Have fun."

"You bet we will."

The last items stowed aboard were my duffel bag,

the rifle and machete (both wrapped in the blanket), and Penny's blue pack with the two grand she'd heisted from her old man's safe. I no longer had any reservations about dipping into that cash reserve if the need arose. Theft was small-time compared to, say, abduction of a minor. Not to mention abandoning a rental vehicle and stealing a rental boat.

The latter was accomplished by heading into the channel, veering behind a mangrove key, and steering a northeast course, parallel to the big keys linked by the highway. The bass boat didn't handle like *Bushwhacked*, my custom guide boat, nor did it have the power. The spray dodger came in handy, though. Penny hunkered down behind it, wearing an orange life jacket as we skimmed over light, sun-sparkled waters the color of Coke-bottle glass. There was a blob of sunscreen on her nose.

"You just keep your fingers crossed," I shouted over the roar of the outboard. "Pray we don't get rained on!"

As if the possibility of rain was our biggest problem. I veered the boat out around Big Torch, Big Pine, and No Name Key. Without binoculars it was hard to be sure, but it looked like the northbound traffic was backed up all the way from the Seven Mile Bridge. By now Sheriff Whiddon and his boys had to be the objects of a collective death wish. All those irate motorists steaming behind their wheels. Chances were that the pearl-handled revolvers and the reflecting shades would spook a few dope-runners into dumb-ass moves before the day was out, and the roadblock operation wouldn't be a total loss, from the law's point of view.

Somehow, though, I didn't think they'd be sending me a thank-you note. Not that I'd left a forwarding address, at least not one that could be readily discerned.

I hadn't mentioned Grandma to Nel Kerry. Hadn't considered her a real possibility until he erased all the other options by deciding to return Penny to her father.

It was midafternoon when I found the channel to one of the larger marinas on the Gulf side of Marathon, halfway up the string of islands. No one paid any attention as I tied off the boat at the dock.

"You get some of those sandwiches out and eat, young lady. I've got a couple of errands and then we'll be out of here."

"I'd rather go with you."

I said, "Flattered, I'm sure. By now they may be looking for a man and a red-haired girl, traveling alone. I doubt any of the marinas would have been notified yet, but you never know. You stay with the boat. Anybody comes along and wants to strike up a conversation, play dumb, okay?"

The visor bobbed. I hurried up to the chandlery and bought two five-gallon fuel containers, binoculars, and a book of navigational charts that included Florida Bay, from the Lower Keys to Everglades City. Items that would have aroused suspicion at the marina where we'd rented the boat.

Next on the agenda was a call to Stanley Horn, intrepid reporter. He was not at his desk but was believed to be in the building. Would I wait while he was paged? That was difficult, since the pay phone had gobbled all my coins. Could Mr. Horn please return my call to the pay-phone number, and please stress that it was an emergency.

"What is the nature of the emergency, sir?"

"Tell Stan I've got a scoop for him."

"A what, sir?"

"You know, one of those stop-the-press items."

"Nobody stops the presses, sir," the voice said, amused. "That's only in the movies."

"Will you have him call me right back?"

"I'll get the message to him, sir. Scoop, ha-ha, now how do you spell that?"

Yuk-yuk. I waited near the phone, counting off minutes. Was about to give up on Stanley damned Horn when the damn thing rang.

"T. D. Stash, I presume?"

"How'd you guess?"

"Lower Keys exchange. I looked it up."

I told him about paying a visit to Bert Hamper and finding that someone had helped him shuffle off his mortal coil.

"Hamper is what?" Horn said.

"Deceased. Dead. Gone but not forgotten."

"And you say he came into a large sum of money? How did you determine that?"

"I paced off his new yacht. Retails in the mid-six figures. All the extras, including a cockpit stereo system. Guess what old Bert was listening to when his clock got stopped? I'll give you a hint, he was a Sinatra fan."

Horn sighed. " 'Strangers in the Night.' "

"Bingo," I said.

"I'll have to go to my editor with this. Maybe we can work something up on the money trail. Any progress in locating the little girl?"

I told him, very briefly, what had transpired. He was, to put it mildly, interested. So interested he wanted me to come up to Miami and tell the story in person to his editor. Then, of course, I could surrender the both of us to the police.

"Sounds like a lot of fun," I said. "Maybe some other time. Tra-la, I've got to run."

"Wait just a sec—"

I hung up. Had a sudden sick feeling upon realizing I had given away a pay-phone number that would be a big help in tracing my movements. Then decided that a *Herald* reporter would likely elect to protect a source, even if they no longer stopped the presses.

Penny wasn't there when I got back to the boat. I leapt in and checked under the spray dodger. No little red-haired girls. Blood started to pound in my head.

"I had to go."

I turned. Penny was standing behind me on the dock. She'd had to use the bathroom. Was that okay? Yes, of course it was okay. I handed her the sandwich she hadn't eaten.

"You stay right here on the dock while I get the extra tanks gassed up. And I want to see teeth marks in that sandwich. I'm the captain and you're the mate, and that means you have to eat if I give the order. Understood?"

"Yes, sir," she said, with just the ghost of a smile.

I topped off the tanks at the fuel dock, paying cash. If the kid at the pumps remembered anything, it would be a wise-ass fisherman, traveling alone, who happened to mention he was heading for Key West.

Penny was waiting right where I'd left her. The sandwich was gone. She had a look in her eye that made me suspicious.

I said, "Did you eat that or drop it overboard? A fib will make your nose grow."

"I kind of dropped it."

"Right. Into the boat with you."

Penny crouched behind the spray dodger, out of sight, until we cleared the marina channel. I set the controls at neutral and let the outboard idle. Penny actually smiled when I handed her another sandwich.

"You don't have to enjoy it but you do have to eat it. Every bite. That's an order."

While she nibbled at the sandwich, I unfurled the chartbook and plotted a course that would take us straight across Florida Bay to Flamingo, outpost to the Everglades. A distance of some thirty miles, depending on tide, drift, and wind. Once we made Flamingo, the next step would be to rent or buy a vehicle and drive the rest of the way to Marco Island, find Penny's grandmother, bring Jake Bonner to justice, clear my name, and let Penny live happily ever after.

That was the plan. I figured it might take a few days to tie up all the loose ends. A few days, or maybe the rest of my life.

"Penny, it'll be near sundown by the time we get where we're going. When you finish that sandwich put on some more sunscreen. Then pile the cushions under you because it's going to be a bumpy ride. You feel the least bit chilly, wrap up in that blanket. Now, what do you say?"

"Okay?"

"You say, 'Aye aye, Captain!' "

"Aye aye, Captain."

It was silly, but I thought it might help to make a game of it. The long, grueling boat-ride game. The let's-find-Gramma game. The let's-put-Dad-in-jail game.

12

WE raised the Number 10 buoy and turned up the channel into Flamingo just as a burnt-orange twilight settled over the Gulf. It had been a hard, choppy ride, with only one pause at the midpoint to switch over the fuel tanks. Penny bore it without complaint. This was remarkable, considering that many of the give-'em-hell anglers I've guided would have been whining to go home after twenty minutes under similar conditions.

The swampy heat of the rainy season became apparent as soon as I slowed the boat down to enter the waterway. The air was thick, humid, droning with the swarms of insects that came out to greet us. Dragonflies arrived first—the big, long-range bombers—followed by steep-diving mosquitoes. The Blue Angels of bloodsucker world. Funny how you forget about the insect factor until the first bite. Then it all comes back and that's what you remember most about the Everglades: the background static of a billion buzzing bug things.

Flamingo is situated at the southern tip of the Florida Peninsula, outpost to the Everglades. It used to be an isolated fishing village, accessible only by water. Poaching was a way of life for generations. At the turn of the century the cash crop was exotic bird feathers destined for mademoiselle's chapeau. Later gator skin was in vogue, and the slaughter of the big reptiles brought them to the verge of extinction. Nowadays the sleepy little village is hooked up to the Ingraham Highway, and most of the natives make a living from the National Park, one way or another. Birdwatchers and sports fishermen arrive in about equal numbers, drawn by thirty-five hundred square miles of subtropical wilderness. Creatures abound here, including the pink-winged Phoenicopteridae for which the village is named.

"It's beautiful," Penny said. She was crouched in the bow, oblivious to the insects and the heat, gazing into the eerie, primeval place where the great grassy swamp gradually melted into the sea. "Are we going to stay here?"

"Just for the night."

I made directly for the fuel dock and replenished the gas, out of habit. Didn't bother with the ploy of keeping Penny out of sight. We were a world away from Key West and Coral Gables. There wasn't a Shake'n Jake disco for many a mile. If Nel Kerry discovered that I had rented a boat—and I assumed he would, sooner or later—the logical conclusion would be that we were island-hopping up to the mainland.

Most of the gear I left in the boat, ready to transfer to a rental vehicle in the morning. The duffel bag and Penny's pack came along with us to the Flamingo Inn. The mosquito season had cut down on the influx of tourists and we had our pick of rooms.

The clerk, a languorous youth wearing an Everglades T-shirt, transferred his squint from a small television screen to me and remarked, "Long ride, huh?"

"Lord, yes," I sighed. "Flight out of Atlanta was delayed three hours. They lost our luggage, naturally. Lucky we had a little something in the carryon. Then, wouldn't you know it, the AC on the tour bus up and died. One heck of a long day, hey, Kitten?" I said, tousling Penny's hair.

"Sure was, Dad."

The clerk smiled thinly. "Down for the fishing?"

"You bet."

"Booking a guide?" he said, reaching for a brochure.

"Maybe tomorrow. Right now all I want is a shower and a cool room."

He handed me the guide brochure with the room key. Polite but persistent. I paid cash, registering as William Budd, of Athens, Georgia. The clerk turned back to his television.

The unit was on the ground floor, as requested, and facing away from the parking lot. The air inside was sufficiently cool, the shower was sufficiently hot. The twin beds had the standard motel mattresses, not as firm as I like, but adequate. In truth, the bay crossing had taken the starch out of me. I could have slept on the bare ground.

Not that I planned it that way.

I washed up first, donned clean duds from the duffel bag, and went out alone to pick up a change of clothes for Penny. Not being tuned in to what was fashionable for nine-year-old girls that year, I let the pretty brunette who ran the general store pick out a pair of powder-blue overalls and a couple of T-shirts with variations on the park logo. Pajamas, kids or otherwise, were not available. The brunette suggested that I select something from the après-swim display.

"Nothing for après swamp, I take it?"

"Pardon me, sir?"

I said, "Never mind," and remembered, on the way out, to buy an economy-sized dispenser of bug repellent.

When I got back to the room, Penny was gone. Not in the bathroom, not under the bed or in the closet. Gone. I looked for the blue pack. It was shoved into the bottom drawer of the motel bureau. So she hadn't decided to light out on her own.

Heart thumping, I dropped onto one of the beds and decided to give her five minutes. Didn't take anywhere near that long.

Penny walked in the door, serene as could be, holding a small green snake. "Look what I found, T.D. I mean Dad. Right under that first palmetto by the sidewalk."

"You're not afraid of snakes?"

She shook her head and let the nasty little thing writhe in her hands.

"I am," I said firmly. "Kindly remove that viper from the premises."

"It's not a viper. Just a plain old green snake."

I jerked my thumb at the door.

Penny sighed, whispered a few words of encouragement to the creature, and released it into the grass outside the door. When she came back in we had a little talk about her not leaving the room without telling me first, and about the inadvisability of introducing legless reptiles into my presence.

"Lizards, bats, crickets, spiders, cockroaches, fine. I do, however, insist on a snake-free environment."

Penny said, "That's a phobia, you know."

"Yes, and I cherish it. Now, go take a shower and see if these new clothes fit. What do you say?"

"Aye, aye, Captain."

Say what you like, I run a tight ship. The evening rations were takeout cheeseburgers, courtesy of the motel restaurant. I got Penny, at her request, something reputed to be a nondairy shake. Just plain coffee for me, thanks. Penny drank all of the shake and ate most of a cheeseburger and then fell soundly asleep on her bed, still clutching the empty shake container.

I managed to take the cup away without waking her and covered her with a thin blanket. After adjusting the air-conditioner, I carried the telephone into a corner of the room and called the most cantankerous, disreputable man I knew.

" 'Lo, Mutt," I said, keeping my voice low.

"T.D.! Sumbitch we in *big* trouble, bubba."

"What's a matter? Nel Kerry come around and rough you up?"

Mutt snorted. I could hear the television set buzzing in his small trailer. "All he did he ax me where you gone, and I said damned if I know. Which was the truth. It ain't cops I'm worried about, though. Not after what I just seen on the TV."

"What did you see?" I demanded, sitting up straighter. I glanced at Penny, whose breath was coming deep and regular.

Mutt said, "Hey, T.D., you know a couple of ugly-looking hombres call 'emselves Ellis and Orrin Cullen?"

"They were on TV?"

"No, not them. But they was on the docks not more'n an hour after you left. One of the bastards pulled a gun on me, said if I didn't take 'em to you they'd shoot me and stuff me down a gator hole. Leastways that's what I think he said. Man got a strange way of talkin'."

"Probably tough to understand if you come from New Jersey, hey, Mutt?"

"Where's that?" he said, not missing a beat. "Out near Utah, is it? No, that's New-vada. I'm serious, T.D., them Cullen brothers is bad news. They gunnin' for you."

I could hear him puffing on a cigar as he talked. So he hadn't run out of Cubans. "Those two thugs haven't got a clue, Mutt," I said. "They have no way of tracking me now, and it's a great big state."

"Not big enough, bubba," he said. "Not when you on the TV."

"What?"

"That's what I been tryin' to tell ya. You all made the evening news out of Miami. Kidnapping charge. How you're armed and dangerous, and you're a suspect in a death by arson, and you abducted a mentally unstable child. They flashed a picture of the little girl and they got one of you, too. Looked like maybe you were drunk when it got took. Gave you kind of a criminal appearance."

"Son of a bitch."

"Oh, yeah," Mutt said. "They got the FBI involved, too. Seems like that fella Bonner went and told the feds you was demanding ransom for his little girl. You ain't, I take it?"

"Hell, no."

"Tell me where to meet up with you, T.D. You ain't the only one around here can be armed and dangerous if he has a mind to."

I remembered, with a sudden jolt, that the desk clerk had been watching television when we registered. I said, "Gotta go, Mutt. I'll call again when I can. Be ready."

"Anytime, bubba. Oh, almost forgot. Lil Cashman

made me promise if I heard from you I was to say give yourself up. So give yourself up. There, I said it. Only thing, if you *are* so inclined, make sure it ain't no Cullen brother you give up to."

I tried to wake Penny. She was all the way out and did not respond. Not surprising, considering what she had been through in the last twenty-four hours. Under other circumstances I would have envied her deep, comalike sleep. As it was, I left her on the bed and went out into the heat of the night. From the corner of the motel wing I had a line of sight to the entrance. Light spilled out from the glassed-in area of the registration desk. No movement inside and no vehicles in the vicinity.

Maybe the squinty-eyed kid behind the desk didn't watch the six-o'clock news. The thought was of some comfort until I started counting up the other people who might have sighted us. The attendant at the marina, for instance. The pretty brunette at the general store who had helped me select clothing for a girl, age nine. The counter help at the restaurant. Anyone else who might recall seeing an adult male and a small, red-haired girl in the vicinity of the only motel in town.

Too many people. Someone was bound to catch the news report and draw the correct conclusion.

I went back into the room. Penny was sleeping as soundly as ever. I packed my things into the duffel bag, leaving the .38 on top where it was readily available. Then I picked up Penny and managed to hook on to the duffel bag handle with my fingers. We were at the door before I remembered that she'd stashed her lucky backpack under the bed. Somehow I retrieved that without quite dropping the kid.

The night was dark, hot, and dominated by swarms

of mosquitoes. Which may have explained why the village streets were deserted. I got down to the marina without encountering another soul. Penny stirred as I laid her into the bottom of the boat and smeared her face, neck, and hands with insect repellent.

"Mama," she murmured, and then fell soundly asleep the instant I slipped a cushion under her head.

I unwrapped the mooring lines and eased the boat away from the dock. I didn't start up the outboard, not right away. We just drifted into the waterway while I waited for inspiration. Plan A had been to flee up the Overseas Highway. Plan B had been to cross Florida Bay to Flamingo and then drive overland to Marco Island. I hadn't bothered with a Plan C.

What I finally did was give up the idea of plans, alphabetically arranged or otherwise. We would simply proceed to Grandma's house by whatever means available. Such as the Wilderness Waterway. Sensible folk enter the waterway at Everglades City and drift south through some hundred miles of shallow river and mangrove swamps and on into the vastness of Whitewater Bay, where at last the bay empties through a back-country canal at Flamingo. Sensible folk go with the flow.

Not being a sensible folk, I got out an oar and started paddling against the current.

13

THE motel was visible from the canal. By a process of logical deduction I was able to conclude, therefore, that the canal was likewise visible from the motel. Which meant that the big park ranger with the sidearm and the flashlight might see the white hull of a passing boat if he happened to turn and look toward the canal.

The ranger had arrived at the motel in a Jeep, accompanied by the pretty brunette who had sold me the new blue overalls for Penny. It was nice to know that somebody in Flamingo watched the news and was prepared to do their civic duty by notifying the rangers that a notorious kidnapper was prowling the village, buying insect repellent, and making wise remarks about items of clothing. The brunette remained by the Jeep, nervously puffing on a cigarette and swatting at mosquitoes while the ranger went into the office.

I kept paddling. Wouldn't do to start up the outboard and draw attention to the fact that some damn fool was heading upriver at night, with thunder rumbling in the distance.

The ranger came out of the office. The squinty clerk said something to the brunette, who nodded. Then the clerk pointed to the wing of the building where Penny and I had been briefly in residence. He handed the ranger something. A room key, perhaps. The ranger fumbled at his hip, unbuttoning his holster. A reasonable man would want to be prepared when confronting an armed and dangerous fugitive.

The three of them started for the room, the ranger in the lead and the clerk bringing up the rear, prudent fellow that he was. I dug in with the oar, trying to make progress against the invisible flow of the black canal. Getting nowhere slow. When the trio turned the corner of the building, I decided to risk starting the motor.

In the still air it sounded like a string of firecrackers exploding. I expected the ranger to come running around the corner with his gun drawn. I expected bright lights to flash all around the village. I expected sirens and bells and whistles.

What actually happened was . . . nothing much. I throttled down and steered through the middle of the canal, leaving the motel and the ranger and the pretty, civic-minded brunette back there in the steamy dark. There were no shouts or warning shots. The ranger would be checking out the room and wondering if the brunette had her story straight. The desk clerk would be recalling my mention of arriving by bus. There was every chance that the ranger would not hear from the dock attendant at the marina until morning. It was probable that even as I entered the mouth of Whitewater Bay, roadblocks were being set up on the Ingraham Highway.

We had, if our luck held, an eight-hour head start. More than enough time, I hoped, to vanish into the vast wilderness. The Seminoles had evaded capture for generations. All I needed was forty-eight hours to reach Marco Island.

The first stroke of lightning lit up the sky when we were about a mile into the bay. I counted, calculating that the storm was ten miles to the west. When the next bolt struck, slightly closer, Penny woke up crying.

"Don't!" she cried. "No! No!"

It took only a minute or two to calm her down. Not bad, considering she'd fallen asleep on a bed in an air-conditioned room and awakened in an open boat under a hot, starless sky.

"Did my dad find us?" she wanted to know.

"No," I said. "Nothing like that. I just decided it would be safer if we left at night."

More rumbles from the storm.

"I'm not scared," Penny said. "Are you?"

"Not a bit."

"Only snakes," she said sleepily.

"Only snakes," I agreed.

The idea was to get across the wide-open bay and into the protective foliage of the Snake River before daybreak. It was a good idea; it just didn't work out that way. Fat pellets of warm rain came down moments before the wind kicked up, running before the storm. I turned the boat and ran with it, hoping I would be able to see the shoreline before we ran aground. I did, courtesy of the lightning flashes. A hummock of cedar trees, with mangroves thick along the water's edge. In the flashes of light the mangrove branches looked like brittle fingers piercing a pool of black ink.

The wind got stronger. Small wavelets began to slosh at the mangrove roots. I found an opening through the thicket and bumped the bow of the boat up on solid ground. The rain was coming heavy.

Naturally I'd neglected to buy ponchos at the general store.

I did, however, have a flashlight. Using it to fill in between flashes, I unfastened the canvas spray dodger and carried Penny into the stand of cypress trees. I spread the canvas over the lowest of the overhanging branches. As shelters went, it wasn't exactly the Hilton, but it kept out the worst of the downpour.

The thunderheads came through in succession, noisy and wet. In the intervals between storms I went back to the boat and got cushions and life jackets and made a lumpy platform above the wet ground. I put the blanket over Penny not because it was cold—if anything the night air seemed hotter after the rain—but as a barrier against the swarms of mosquitoes that descended every time the deluge let up.

So far we were having a spiffy time. It was just what a traumatized child needed: a night in the Everglades, donating blood to the insects. While she slept, somewhat fitfully, I stared into the darkness and tried not to think about Connie Geiger.

"You can stay the night if you want. In my bed or elsewhere, your choice."

Leery of rekindling an old intimacy, I had chosen to go home to my own bed. Too numbed by road weariness and cheap rum to hear what she was really saying:

"I'm frightened. Please stay and help."

It wasn't only the mosquitoes and stormy weather that kept me awake. It was the maybes. Maybe if I'd noticed the tail who followed me from Key Largo . . . Maybe if I'd stayed with Connie . . . Maybe if . . .

The bite of the maybe is worse than any bug bite.

There is no repellent but sleep, and sleep was not available.

Dawn was a pale-yellow fog drifting over the mangroves. Penny awoke cranky and sullen. The green eyes looked at me with suspicion. Who was this bleary, unkempt adult who drags little girls into the swamp and makes them sleep on wet boat cushions?

The sullenness melted into a radiant smile when she saw the surprise Mother Nature had arranged for her enjoyment. Three small gators had come ashore, seeking refuge from the storm. Unlike yours truly, they had no trouble falling asleep and seemed in no rush to move out of the way as we headed for the boat. Blinking cold, lethargic eyes and yawning their cute little gator jaws.

"Neat," Penny said.

"Yeah, great," I said. "The bad news is that if bitten, I would probably survive."

"They hardly *ever* bite."

I was grateful that she didn't want to actually handle the damn things. The gators slithered out of my way as I stamped around, carrying gear back to the boat. Penny sat in the bow, content to watch as the beasts slipped into the water and became floating logs. Apparently there's nothing like a few baby alligators when it comes to lifting a girl's spirits.

The sun was high enough to burn through the malarial mists by the time I found the marker indicating the entrance to the Shark River estuary. I was glad to be out of the open bay and into a place where we could duck for cover in the mangroves at a moment's notice. I had no idea how extensive the search for us might be. Would it be confined to roadblocks, or would they—they being the various sheriffs departments cooperating, I had to assume, with the feds—push for a full-scale manhunt, with air support?

The answer on air support became obvious shortly before noon. I had kept to the middle of the shallow river, running at two-thirds throttle to conserve fuel. Making about eight knots' headway against the leisurely current. That was fast enough to bring some relief from the heat and the bugs. Except for an occasional heron feeding at the mangrove roots, we had the waterway pretty much to ourselves. In four hours I passed only a single canoe, laden with two intrepid paddlers draped in mosquito netting. Penny, warned of the approach, stayed out of sight until we cleared the next bend. It was she who heard the chopper first and pointed it out.

"Over that way, just above the trees," she said. "It looks like a red-and-white dragonfly."

Well, yes. The coast-guard markings did give it that look. The helicopter was several miles distant, flying a recon pattern over the Cape Sable area. I tracked it through the binoculars and decided it might come too close for comfort. We would have lunch undercover at the head of the Shark River. I found a suitable place to beach near the slough and used the machete to fell enough mangrove branches to camouflage the boat.

With the boat hidden, we made for a stand of dwarf cypress. It was slightly cooler in the shade of the dense Spanish moss that dripped from the trees. We ate stale sandwiches and the mosquitoes ate us. The repellent was an appetizer. Penny was stoic, brushing the black clots of bugs from her hair. I was more the slap-and-growl type.

An hour later the helicopter passed overhead. The

prop wash shook the cypress trees, displacing a few billion insects, and continued around the bend into the seaward leg of the waterway. Ten minutes later the sound was barely discernible above the background whine of the bugs.

"We'll give it another half-hour," I said.

Penny put her finger to her lips. She was looking behind me. I slipped my hand into the duffel bag and wrapped my fingers around the .38. A pair of yellow eyes stared back at me through the ferns. Cat eyes. I eased the revolver out of the bag.

The eyes blinked and were gone. The ferns shivered. There was the briefest glimpse of fur. Penny sighed. She had been holding her breath.

"Well?" I said to her. "You're the wildlife expert. What was it?"

"I don't know."

"I vote for bobcat," I said. "Or anyhow a feline-type critter."

Penny grinned and said, "Don't you just love it here?"

I said, "Aren't you scared of anything?"

The smile vanished like the yellow cat eyes.

"Not animals," she said.

Me and my big mouth.

From the slough area it was another twelve miles of big, winding bends to the Gulf. Now the current was behind us, running to the sea. The hardwood hammocks gave way to a world of low mangroves, as far as the eye could see. Ibis birds stood by the mangrove roots at intervals of a few hundred yards, like small white sentries at attention as we paraded by.

I put Penny in charge of helicopter detection. She took the duty very seriously indeed, scanning the wide mangrove horizons with the binoculars. How effective that was, considering the size of the glasses and the smallness of her hands, was beside the point. Better to keep her busy—and she'd already proved that her eyes were remarkably sharp.

We never did spot the chopper again. We saw something a whole lot worse, though, not long after the river emptied us into the shallow waters of the Gulf.

I had just made the turn to the north, intending to run fairly close inshore. The next section of the inner waterway was a few miles ahead. Once there, I would have to decide whether to go back into the protective swamp, with its winding passages, or risk a straight, all-night run to Everglades City, where I planned to refuel for the last leg of the journey. It was all mapped out in my head when I happened to glance out to sea. Suddenly I lost interest in maps and plans.

"Get down," I said. Penny dropped into the bottom of the boat. "Okay, now hand me the binocs. Keep it low."

There was a sizable sport-fishing machine running on a parallel course, less than a mile offshore. Kicking up a nice rainbow of spray. Sleek, seaworthy lines and a whole lot of varnished mahogany. A lovely, all-business design I happened to be familiar with, having seen a new one up close only a few days before. It was a Rybovich 55, just like the Rybovich 55 Jake Bonner kept tethered to the dock at his Coral Gables home.

Jake Bonner wasn't driving his big expensive boat, though. There was a Swamp Thing at the wheel and another up on the flying bridge. Ellis and Orrin Cullen, the bad-news brothers. Heading north for

Marco Island and Grandma's house and hoping to find us on the way. They hadn't gotten a good look at us yet, or the bows of the Rybovich would have been aiming our way, of that I was convinced.

"You hang on down there," I said to Penny. "We're going to pick up the pace."

I opened the throttle and tried to look like an angler heading for home. Veering ever so slightly toward the opening to the inland waterway. About a quarter-mile from the entrance I risked a nonchalant-type glance over my shoulder.

The course were no longer parallel. They were converging. Rapidly.

I skidded the boat into a tight turn, cutting close to the navigational stakes. Sliding behind the first thin cover of mangroves that presented itself. It was right around then that they commenced firing.

14

IF the Cullen brothers knew how to read a chart, it didn't show. By trying to follow our little outboard they ran their big fishing machine into the mud shoal that jutted into the channel. Boys will be boys. The top of the flying bridge was just visible above the intervening mangroves as I gunned it upriver, trying to put at least a few miles between us before they kedged themselves off the mud bank and followed.

The wild shots had been fired from a high-powered rifle. Any doubts I might have had about Jake Bonner's intentions were erased by the flat, ugly noise of lead hitting our wake. Of all the decisions I'd made lately, taking Penny was the rightest, the best. There would be no late-night maybes on that score.

When we were clear, Penny said, "That was my dad."

"Not quite," I said. "A couple of creeps who work for him. Great big hairy devils. Talk funny."

"Oh," she said, her face going still. "Them."

Them. An apt description. Right to the point. Just plain old *them*.

"They're kin of Lee Ann's," Penny said. "The one with the bite mark on his ear used to drive me to school sometimes."

"Bite mark?"

She nodded. "Dad said it was a real convenience, so's he could tell who was who. They kind of came with Lee Ann."

"You mean that's when they started working for your father? After he met Lee Ann?"

She nodded. Clearly it was not one of her favorite topics of conversation. It was an interesting item of information—that the Cullen brothers were somehow related to Lee Ann—but I didn't see quite how it fit into the whole scheme. Idle speculation. What counted now was getting clear.

I turned the binoculars back over to Penny, although there was nothing to see but sky and mangrove, mangrove and sky. I kept glancing back as we whipped through the river bends, ready to drive the boat into a thicket if the tall flying bridge showed over the foliage astern.

Daylight was rapidly fading. I tried to decide if darkness would be an advantage, and to whom. The Cullen boys were swamp men, born and bred. That they were skilled trackers was not in doubt. The best that could be hoped for was that nightfall would be neutral.

The idea of being overtaken on the waterway was something I did not care to contemplate. Better, I thought, to go deeply to cover. Five or so miles upriver the mangroves gave way to broad areas of saw grass interspersed with hardwood hammocks and shallow islands. The light was fading to that shade of thin, airbrushed orange that is peculiar to the glades. It was time to make a move.

I picked out a nearby hammock and cut the motor while we were still in the channel.

"What's wrong?" Penny asked.

"Nothing's wrong. We're about to disappear, is all."

With the motor up, I did something every keys fishing guide knows how to do in his sleep, if necessary: pole a boat through shallow water. The idea was not to leave a propeller trail through the saw grass. As I pushed into the shallows, walking the boat with an oar, I had Penny pull the grass back into place.

"That a girl," I said. "Fluff it up. Any blade you notice that's bent or broken, tell me and I'll cut it off with the knife."

Poling had another advantage. I could listen for the whine of the Rybovich's big engines. So long as there was relative quiet, we could take our time covering the faint trail that even a shallow hull makes as it passes through saw grass.

The hammock was about three hundred yards from the channel, and it took a while to get there, careful as I was being with the grass. Setting my sneakered feet down into the muck, I walked the boat around to the back of the hammock, where it couldn't be seen from the waterway. Penny unloaded the gear while I selected green branches to camouflage the hull. When I was done, it looked like part of the hammock, just another lump of rotting leaves and vegetation.

With the boat covered and the gear transferred to a thick stand of hardwoods, it was hurry sundown. The darker the better. I loaded the Ruger and buttoned a box of 30-06 shells in my shirt pocket. I kept the duffel bag close by, with the .38 just inside the zipper, and dropped a dozen revolver shells in my pants pocket.

Penny looked somberly at the firearms without comment.

We ate again. Penny wanted to ration the water and I saw no harm in that.

"I read you can get real sick from drinking brackish water," she said, pouring my portion into a tin cup. "Sometimes the salt can make you see things that aren't there."

"You read a lot, don't you, Penny?"

"Too much, my dad says. Before Mom died, he was always telling her what a know-it-all I was. Kidding, like."

Old Shake'n Jake was quite the kidder. Sending his goons after us was another example of his sense of humor. I went to the edge of our little hiding place and crouched, pulling back a few strands of moss. The band of indigo-blue twilight was being rapidly overtaken by dark smudges. Thick clouds were coming in from the west, ensuring a moonless, starless night. Hurray for clouds!

"We're going to be okay here, Penny," I said, rigging up the canvas cover while a little twilight remained.

"I guess we can't build a fire, huh?"

"Not tonight, no. We're invisible, remember?"

We sat quietly, side by side, sharing the last of the insect repellent. Either the mosquitoes were sated or the stuff was finally beginning to work. Probably it helped to be unwashed.

"What about tomorrow?" Penny wanted to know.

I had no ready answer. Getting through the night was no problem. We were adequately sheltered and camouflaged. What happened when daylight came around depended on the Cullen brothers. If they got off the mud bank and elected to stay in the river, waiting to flush us out, escape would be difficult, if not impossible. We had food and water enough for a few days, no more.

Truth was, I didn't know about tomorrow. I made reassuring noises, though, and after a time Penny fell asleep with her head in my lap. Trusting me the way a cat will trust to land on its feet. It is a grave responsibility, to be trusted by a child. Grave enough to keep me wide awake.

Sitting there blinking in the dark, I was again amazed by the intense variety of noises emitted by critters from the swamp. Screeching birds, thrumming cicadas, tree frogs, bullfrogs, crickets, engines.

Wait a minute. Back it up. Engines? Gasoline engines? Yes indeed! The throaty *wuga-wuga* sound of paired eight-cylinder power plants at low rev.

I eased Penny onto the cushions and crawled to the edge of the cypress trees. A searchlight was sweeping the waterway. It passed over our hideaway and continued to the opposite side of the river.

I heard a voice pitched slightly higher than the engines. Couldn't make out the words, but it wasn't hard to imagine what they were discussing:

"See anything Ellis?" "No'sum, Orrin, Ah don't."

After staring for a while, I could see part of the cockpit, faintly illuminated by the binnacle light. The roving spotlight was mounted on the fly bridge. I surmised that one brother was steering while the other manipulated the powerful light. Shooting out the spotlight was possible, but it would reveal our proximity, pinpoint our location. At dawn the hairy troops would come ashore, a two-man invasion army.

I decided to let the boys play with their light. Maybe they thought they'd stun us with it, like jackrabbits. Every now and then a distinct word or phrase would carry over the low throb of the engines.

". . . go on ahead now, bubba."

". . . an old gator hole, nearby the head, ain't nothin'."

". . . just a runnin' scared."

The big boat slipped on by. The voices became fainter, the pitch of the engines changed. They cleared the next bend in the river. All I could see was the spotlight. Suddenly it stopped moving.

"Sumbitch!"

That was distinct enough. So were the next few phrases.

"Back her off a there, Ellis."

"She hard aground. Shee-it!"

The engines cranked up to a roar. The spotlight quivered but did not shift position. With the props turning that fast, the big V-bottom Rybovich would either dig itself deeper into the mud or snap a shaft.

"Sumbitch. Who gonna swim out and set that kedge anchor? Ain't me, bubba, not *this* time."

I was getting better at deciphering their thick, swamp-cracker drawl. Probably the result of osmosis, or mosquito bite. I crouched there in the cypress, not particularly thrilled to have the Cullens as neighbors for the night, while the brothers argued about who would go into the water to set the anchor, so the boat could be winched off the mud bank.

"Ain't me, Orrin. You go, or we wait for sunup."

"Shee-it. Ain't no gators in that hole."

"Go on, then."

"Shee-it."

They seemed to be stuck on shee-it. Neither of them anxious to climb into the black water. Too much like taking a bath, probably, and they were not, from appearance, frequent bathers. They were still arguing when I crawled back into the cypress stand and woke Penny.

"Don't say a word," I whispered. "Quiet as a mouse and you'll be plenty safe. Okay?"

I felt her head nod.

"We're going back to the boat," I whispered. "Just hang on."

I carried her to the boat and uncovered it, taking care not to rustle the branches. The brothers were too busy bitching at each other to notice anything that subtle, but what the heck, better to play it safe. I stowed the gear in the boat and made it clear that Penny was to make herself comfortable in the bottom and go back to sleep, if possible. The tension I sensed in her made that unlikely.

"Everything will be okay," I whispered. "Promise."

The next move was going to be tricky. I might pole the boat out into the channel without attracting attention. Then again I might not. If the spotlight found us, we'd be easy meat for the high-caliber rifles.

I decided that, like it or not, I would have to pay a visit to the Cullens. Just to be neighborly.

The water was cooler than the air. Refreshing, almost. If you ignored the concept of water moccasins and alligators and leeches. Although the water was probably too brackish here for leeches. Leaving only the snakes and the gators.

I had blackened my face with mud. Suspended from a piece of line around my neck was the .38, more or less sealed in a Zip-loc sandwich bag. Just for giggles I'd strapped Mutt's Ka-bar knife to my ankle. That way if a gator got me by the leg, it might break a tooth or at the very least suffer indigestion.

It was so black out there, I had to feel for the water. Slogging along the mud bank, waist-deep, to avoid unnecessary splashing. I'd debated shedding my sneakers. Decided to deal with their extra weight rather than feel my bare toes slipping into the goo, and the unnamable things that lived in the goo.

For all I knew, leeches loved brackish water. A scrotum-tightening thought.

On reflection I may have been dwelling overmuch on the things that lived in the water because they were less frightening than the things that lived out of the water, namely the Cullen brothers. Who had switched off the spotlight.

I judged distance and direction by the sound of the engines and the occasional raised voice, as the brothers continued to discuss who would take the kedge anchor into the water, and when. After a while I started to think of them as Sumbitch and Shee-it, rather than Ellis and Orrin. Just a couple of good old boys out on a moonless night, people-hunting.

When I could make out the faint glow of the binnacle light, I slipped into the river. There was a moment of panic as the cooler current tugged, wanting me under. Then I was swimming toward the glow. Dog-paddling, because that seemed the quietest way to go. The closer I got, the more distinct was the conversation.

"They upriver by now, El. Settle down, bubba, set easy. We fetch 'em in Glade City, by and by."

"We winged the sumbitch, maybe."

"Maybe. Maybe not. All I knowed, it nigger black out there. We do back this off'n this mud, we only gonna run't agroun' another place. Best wait for sunup."

Yackety-yack, I thought. Keep talking, boys.

My right hand hit something soft. The mud bank. The shock of it caused me to swallow a gulp of water. It tasted like something a brontosaurus had bathed in after a long hot aeon.

The engines were quite loud now. I became aware of the hot, burbling stream of the wet exhaust. I could no longer see the binnacle glow, which meant I was under the oblique angle of the transom. Very close indeed. I got another taste of the swamp when my forehead bumped into the boarding platform.

I rested there with my elbows up on the platform, getting oriented. I was at the stern. The brothers sounded like they might still be up on the flying bridge. That suited me just fine.

I crawled up onto the platform with infinite care. The churning engines were a comfort, covering any little slips I might make. When I was fully on the platform, I lay on my back and untied the rope around my neck. The Zip-loc bag was slippery and wet. Inside it, the .38 was only slightly damp.

I put the muzzle to my mouth and used my teeth to pull out the wad of paper I'd stuffed in the barrel. Then breathed into it, expelling any water that might be trapped there. A misfire would be embarrassing, to say the least.

In this world of modern complexity, even us Renaissance types can't be expert in everything. For instance, I have only a layman's rudimentary understanding of chemistry and physics. I know that a bullet fires when the charge ignites and rapidly expands, forcing the slug out the muzzle, but I can't say precisely why that happens. Another for-instance. I know that crude oil is "cracked" by a refractory process that produces, at the top of the stack, the thin, volatile liquid we Americans call gasoline—but I don't know exactly how that is accomplished.

One subject I do have expertise in is boats: the design and function thereof, and the process by which they are built. For instance, I happened to know exactly where the fuel tanks would be installed on a Rybovich sport-fishing model. Also—and here's where the real expertise comes in—I knew where the vent caps were located. This is not an item of knowledge useful at universities or on game shows. Years may go by without such wisdom bearing fruit.

But just put yourself on the stern of a vessel while in possession of a handy firearm, and this arcane knowledge of fuel tanks and vent caps can be useful, provided you are willing to destroy an example of the finest Florida craftsmanship. Wrecking the Rybo, then, was the act of a frightened expert. There, that's my excuse.

What I did was crouch at the stern, feel for the vent cap, and unscrew it with great care. Up on the fly bridge the Cullens were still deep in a discussion of the merits of swimming at night in the proximity of a gator hole. I have reason to believe they were more than a little surprised at what happened next.

I braced my legs for a jump, shoved the muzzle of the .38 into the open vent, and fired five slugs of very hot lead into the two-hundred-gallon tank of gasoline. Then I leapt backward into the water and was kicking with adrenalinized enthusiasm before the sound of the final shot faded.

I stayed under as long as I could, stroking hard. Wanting to be as far into the inky blackness as possible in case Ellis or Orrin decided to take a few random shots off the stern. Also not particularly anxious to be in the immediate vicinity when the leaking gasoline reached the critical state when bilge fumes plus spark equals big boom.

I needn't have worried about being fired on. When I came up for air, I could hear the Cullen boys. Their discussion was at a much higher decibel level. Ellis was recommending evacuation, to commence immediately. Orrin expressed himself as follows, "Shee-it! Shee-it! Shee-it!"

You couldn't blame him. He didn't know any better. The fireball, when it came, lit up the sky, and the hot wind of it turned the river water to molten gold, for just that one special instant before the sound of the explosion drove me back under.

15

LIFE never feels so precious as when you've done a remarkably dumb and dangerous thing and survived. By the time I had the boat away from the hammock and heading back down river to the Gulf, I felt as if I'd guzzled a bottle of fine champagne. High and happy and just a teeny bit sick.

The low clouds glowed with reflected flames. More than a few acres of swamp grasslands would be scorched before the fire burned itself out. There was a kind of pleasing symmetry in the explosion. What goes around comes around; what the Cullens had done to Connie had now been done to them.

I did not feel like a killer. Maybe that would come later, when the shock and thrill had worn off. And of course I did not know absolutely that the brothers were dead. Maybe they'd gotten off the boat before the gasoline detonated. I hadn't waited around to inspect the wreckage. I was strictly a blow-it-up-and-run-like-hell man. Rather proud of myself, which may have explained the touch of nausea under the adrenaline high.

When I returned to the hammock, Penny had been hiding in the bottom of the boat as instructed. I hadn't instructed her to aim the rifle at the first person to appear. That was her own idea.

"I'll shoot," she said. "I will."

I was covered with mud and swamp ooze. Looking, no doubt, like a slightly reduced version of a Cullen. Luckily she recognized my voice. As it happened, there wasn't a bullet in the chamber. Still, the incident sparked my adrenaline level that much higher.

Our luck held for the rest of the night. Shortly after we cleared the river mouth into the Gulf, the cloud cover broke. The Gulf was glassy calm. The work lights of the shrimp trawlers looked like strings of carnival lights out in the deep water. Running at full throttle under a racing moon, I fetched up on the Ten Thousand Islands area in less than two hours. From there it was slower going, navigating between the myriad islands until I finally saw the dim lights of Everglades City, population five hundred.

Now five hundred souls doesn't make a city, but you've got to admit it, Everglades Village just doesn't sound right. It is said that Everglades City is what Flamingo would be like if Flamingo had a post office. The urban cave dwellers will have their little jokes. I didn't care about a post office. All I wanted was a pay phone and a gas dock.

I found both items mingled in the form of Newson's Fuel & Bait, which looked like the kind of place Mutt Durgin would run if he'd come ashore there instead of Key West. The bait shack was padlocked and the gas pump shut off, but the pay phone functioned just fine.

I had to let it ring awhile before Mutt answered.

"Are you sober?" I said.

"Sleepin'. That you, T.D.?"

Our conversation was short. Mutt allowed as how

he was open to suggestion. I made a few and he willingly agreed.

"Bubba," he said, "I'm on my way. Color me gone."

It took another hour or so to round up the good old boy who ran the fuel docks. His name, not surprisingly, was Newton B. Newson, or just plain Newt to his customers. Newt was a scrawny, toothless specimen with hound-dog eyes and a droll sense of humor. He assumed I was a drug-runner, and as such, he was happy to serve me, provided I was willing to make it worth his while.

"Had to make an unscheduled detour, eh, bub?" he said, checking me out from behind his screen door.

"You know how it is," I said.

"Yup, I do," he said. "Helluva thing to run low on fuel when the guv'mint boys 'r chasin' yer wake." He peered curiously around the boat as he filled the tanks. Looking for contraband and slightly disappointed not to find any. "Had to dump the stuff, eh?"

I shrugged. "The risk you take when you're out night-fishing."

"Night-fishing!" He chuckled. "What kind of bait you use, bub?"

"The green kind," I said, playing along.

Us big-time smugglers were expected to leave big-time tips for late-night fuel stops. I paid Newt five hundred dollars, which he gave me to know was the price of his silence.

"Thanks," he said, tucking the bills into his belt. "Have a nice day."

Is it any wonder that your average South Florida DEA agent is likely to have a haunted, furtive look about him, when drug-runners are encouraged to have a nice day?

Penny was waiting where I'd left her, sitting at the end of a dock a few hundred yards from Newson's place. I wondered what old Newt would think if he'd known that my contraband was human. Probably glommed me for another five hundred.

When dawn opened like a bloodshot eye over Marco Island, we were anchored near an artificial reef, fishing for jacks. As cover it was pretty thin, but I was too exhausted to think of anything clever. It was all I could do to go through the motions of jigging a lure through the water. There was no place to hide on shore that didn't intrude on the private domains of the resort developers. The only anonymity available was a few hundred yards off the powder-white sands of Marco Beach. Just another dad and his kid. With the baseball cap and the short hair, Penny's gender wasn't obvious from any distance, so it was possible we might be mistaken for father and son. All the better.

Surely no one would expect an armed and dangerous kidnapper to be fishing right out in the open, with his little victim along for the outing?

As the sun rose, a few of the bigger yachts lurched out of the condominium slips in the resort basin. The owners were too busy trying to pilot their gadget-happy craft to pay much attention to a small boat anchored over a pile of submerged truck tires, well out of the channel.

"Will he come?" Penny said, yawning. She had nodded off a couple of times, lulled by the bobbing motion of the anchored boat.

"He'll be here," I said. "By the way, you've got a fish on the line."

It was passing strange that twelve hours after being chased through the Everglades we were anchored off a billion-dollar resort island, calmly reeling in jacks and waiting for a friend. I was getting irritated with the jacks. I kept peeling them off the hook and they kept jumping back on.

"Go 'way," I said to the yellow-bellied thing. "Tell your buddies to quit biting."

Fishing guides are not by nature inclined to lecture fish on the inadvisability of getting caught, but I was so tired that reeling them in was an effort. Finally I managed to hook my lure on a truck tire and left it there. If any of the jacks figured out how to swallow the whole tire, I was planning to drop the rod overboard.

"There's a man on the beach," Penny said. "I think he's waving."

There was indeed a man on the beach. He was wearing tan slacks, a sky-blue blazer with brass buttons, aviator glasses, and a panama hat. He was holding a pair of plimsoles in one hand and waving with the other.

"Is that him?" Penny asked.

"Can't be," I said, reaching for the binoculars. "Impossible."

It was, though. In all the years I'd known Mutt Durgin I'd never seen him wear anything but tattered jeans and T-shirts. The blazer-and-slacks outfit made him look like a normal person, almost. It was disorienting in the extreme.

"Don't look now," I muttered. "But pigs can fly."

I cut the lure, pulled up the anchor, and nosed the boat up on the white beach. Mutt kept back, not wanting to wet the cuffs of the new trousers. Penny and I stumbled ashore.

I said, "Dr. Livingstone, I presume?"

Mutt lifted the sunglasses and squinted. "You all had your breakfast yet?" he said.

That was how we came to be installed in a luxury suite at the Marriott at Marco Beach, overlooking the golf course, the tennis courts, and the green-as-money Gulf.

I stayed under the stinging shower until it felt like I was starting to erode. I rinsed off the essence of swamp; I shaved, brushed my teeth, and found I could look myself in the eye without wincing.

While I was showering Mutt had gone down to the lobby and bought me a new pair of shorts and a pullover shirt with a cute little Marco Beach Hotel & Villa logo on the breast. I wasn't ready to join the blue-blazer set just yet. The look for today was hotel staff, or maybe recreation director.

Mutt and Penny were having breakfast in a dining nook that was only slightly smaller than Mutt's trailer.

"I'm disappointed," I said, affecting disdain as I gazed around the suite. "How come you didn't go for a villa?"

That got me a flinty look and the suggestion that I sit down and have some breakfast and refrain from making snide remarks to someone who had driven all night to help out a pal. Clearly I'd hurt his feelings.

I said, "Take off your hat, Mutt."

"Huh?"

"Do me a favor and take off the hat."

He scowled and took off the panama, holding it carefully by the edges. I leaned over and planted a kiss on the top of his brown, bald head.

"You old coot," I said. "It was a beautiful sight, seeing you there on the beach. I am grateful. Penny is grateful. The suite is terrific, and you look like a million bucks in that getup."

"Man," he muttered, rubbing at the top of his head, "you must be snake-bit."

Over breakfast we exchanged information. I told Mutt about our encounter with the Cullen brothers and he filled me in on the latest from Key West. Nel Kerry had been by to see him not long after Jake Bonner announced to the media that his daughter was being held for ransom.

"The lieutenant's pissed at you for runnin' off and makin' him look foolish, but he ain't buyin' the ransom stuff. For one thing, they know for a fact the fire at Connie's was arson, from the outside, not the inside. From what he tole me, the FBI boys are a little leery of Bonner. Nel said—let me get it right—'The Bureau is just going through the motions.' Like maybe they think Jake is lyin', too."

That was welcome news. Less encouraging was the hundred-thousand-dollar reward Bonner was offering for my arrest.

"That beats the heck out of a deputy sheriff's salary," Mutt said.

In a more perfect world I would have simply called up Mrs. Irene Broscoe of 241 Calusa Point and asked if she would mind an indefinite visit from her granddaughter. Then again, in a more perfect world Penny's mother would still be alive and my only role in her life would be to point out the passing sea turtles.

Trouble was, I didn't know what "going through the motions" might imply to the FBI. I assumed they would be monitoring Jake Bonner's telephone, that there was an agent in place at his home, or nearby. Would the Bureau also go to the trouble and expense of staking out the home of the abducted child's estranged grandmother? It seemed unlikely, but caution compelled me to check out the situation before making a move.

Mutt's advice was this: "The way you can always tell a G-man, his eyes are too close together, okay? Makes 'em look shifty. Also your G-man always looks like he's just had a haircut."

"Thanks, Mutt, I'll keep that in mind."

"I heard they drive Ford sedans," he added. "Big sedans with special motors."

There were no squinty-eyed men driving Ford sedans on Calusa Point. This was Mercedes country, with the occasional rebel making a BMW statement. I parked Mutt's rented Chevy about a quarter-mile from the two-hundred block and got out.

I was armed with a tennis racket. A single, unknown male cruising the ritzy development in a rented car might arouse suspicion. The same fellow on foot, wearing shorts, tennis shoes, and carrying a racket, was obviously harmless. I whistled as I walked, twirling the racket. No one could possibly suspect that I knew more about splitting the atom than the game of tennis.

As Florida developments go, Calusa Point was a quality effort. The homes were solidly built, nicely landscaped. There was a palm-green golf course on one side and a pretty beach of white sand directly on the Gulf. Any residents who felt guilty about displacing the rare bald eagles native to the island had only to look at the rows of artificial nests constructed along the links. They were empty, to be sure, but if the persnickety eagles ever came to their senses, they would return and take up residence in the penthouse bird-condos provided by the developer.

Number 241 was a little more modest than some of the other units. A one-car garage, no outdoor pool or sauna, and alas, no tennis court. I walked briskly by, a guy on his way to a hot game with a buddy's wife, and tried to see what I could see. The answer was, not much. No obvious stakeouts, no squinty-eyed ciphers peering from behind drawn shades. No yardmen clipping the same piece of hedge over and over. No lurkers behind palm trees.

I got to the end of the block, about-faced, and went and rang the bell. *Bing-bong*, kidnapper calling.

"Yes?"

I'd been expecting a standard grandmother. Plump, pink cheeks, checked apron, smelling faintly of apples and cinnamon. She would have gray hair up in a bun. The woman who answered the door was plump only in certain key places, her hair was long and darkly red, and her short culottes showed a lot of firm, ungrandmotherly leg.

" 'Scuse me, miss," I said, saluting her with the tennis racket. "Must have the wrong abode. I'm looking for Mrs. Irene Broscoe."

A thin, wary smile. "You're looking at her."

Indeed I was. "Oh," I said. "I was expecting . . . Never mind. Um, do you by any chance have a granddaughter?"

Irene Broscoe had very expressive gray eyes. They now expressed uncertainty and fear. Her hand went to her throat as she said, in a husky voice, "Is this about Penny?"

I made friendly, tennislike moves with the racket for the benefit of any nosy neighbors who might be watching. "Go back inside and wait," I said. "Do not use the phone. Do not leave any messages. After ten minutes have elapsed, walk down to the private beach and sit on a bench. Any bench will do."

"But who—"

"Tut-tut," I said. "See you in ten."

There was, as I had already ascertained, a restroom facility at the beach. I went into the men's side and peeked through the frosted vent window. From there I could see the row of pastel-pink benches resting in the white sand.

Eleven minutes later Mrs. Broscoe arrived. She had put on a pair of dark glasses and was carrying a shoulder bag. She sat down on the first bench she came to, and began to consume a cigarette with short, nervous puffs.

I walked the perimeter of the beach. Unless the FBI issued cloaks of invisibility, no one had followed Mrs. Broscoe. I walked over to the bench and sat down next to her. She dropped the cigarette in the sand and took off the dark glasses and looked at me, waiting.

"Penny's fine," I said. "She wants to see you."

I don't know how I expected her to react. Tears possibly. Maybe a thankful grandmotherly kiss. Something along those lines. What happened was that Mrs. Broscoe threatened damage to a vital area of my anatomy.

"You'll what?" I said.

"Tell me who you are and what your game is, mister, or I swear to God I'll shoot you right in the balls."

I looked down at her right hand, which was shielded by the handbag. And, yes, by golly, she *was* aiming a snub-nosed .22 pistol at the items in question.

"I'm not armed," I said. It sounded pretty lame. The gun did not waver, nor did Irene Broscoe blink.

"That bastard son-in-law of mine sent you, didn't he? *Didn't he?*"

I had to find a little moisture in my mouth before trusting my voice. "Mrs. Broscoe, I am not one of Jake Bonner's henchmen, and if that gun should happen to go off, I won't be able to take you to Penny. Plus I'll bleed all over this nice white beach."

The eyes told me she'd finally put my face and the image on the six-o'clock news together.

"You're the one who—"

"Yup," I said. "I'm the one who Penny came to when she ran away, convinced her father wanted to do her harm. I'm the one who didn't really believe her until I found out that Shake'n Jake killed his first wife—your daughter Mary Beth. I'm the one who rescued Penny from the cops when they decided to return her to her father's custody. This was after Jake had his goons burn down the house where Penny was staying, killing a dear, sweet woman I was in love with, once upon a time. I'm the one who . . ."

It was right about then that Mrs. Irene Broscoe put away the gun and started to cry.

16

A flock of white pelicans dropped in for lunch. After feeding, they floated a few yards from the beach, squawking and complaining about the small black gull who harassed them from the air.

"Pete was twenty-one when we got hitched," Irene said. "I was seventeen, and pregnant with Mary Beth. He was working as a mason then, wherever he could find a job. We rented this trailer in Indigo Springs. Little nowhere place up the creek from Naples, partway into the Big Cypress Swamp. Mostly poor whites and a few Seminole families. Cheap living in Indigo Springs. See, Pete wanted to save money. He had big plans, even then."

She had put the dark glasses on. Hiding her eyes. Wanting some measure of privacy as she explained how she had come to be a widow on Marco Island.

"We were in that trailer about a year. By then Pete was concrete foreman for a big company and there was enough left over to pick up the mortgage on a little cinder-block ranch. It was about the nicest place in Indigo, and it got a lot nicer. What we did was keep adding on. Pete got his own company going, and he bid for contracts all over the coast, mostly malls. The boom was on, and for a time he had more than a hundred men on the payroll. I took care of the books and the telephone the first few years. Eventually we turned it over to accountants and lawyers. Now, Pete was a hard worker and ambitious, but the plain fact is we got lucky with the business and the land deals and we got rich. We could have moved out of Indigo, but by then it was home."

To hear her tell it, Irene had never been all that enamored with the small, backwater town. There was no social life—at least not any she cared to participate in—and the school was little more than a shanty for the barefoot kids, overseen by instructors of dubious ability.

"I'm not kidding," she said. "When Mary Beth was in fifth grade, she had a teacher who moved her lips when she read. Barely literate. I wanted to send her to a Church school in Naples, but Pete was dead-set against the Church. Said we'd hire a tutor to make up for what she wasn't getting in class. So we did that, we hired a tutor. But—and I could never make Pete understand—it wasn't the teachers I was worried about, bad as they were. It was the boys."

"You have a specific boy in mind?" I asked. The sun was hitting the white beach. Heat eddies rose from the sand and made it seem as if the pelicans were floating on a green mist.

"Not right at first. Pretty soon there was."

I was not terribly surprised to hear that the troublesome lad was Jake Bonner.

"There's a funny kind of thing can happen in a small, isolated place like Indigo Springs. Pete was away a lot, so he didn't see it. I was home with the books and the telephone and Mary Beth, and believe me, I saw it. The kind of trouble I'm talking about is a family thing. In Indigo it was the Bonners and the Cullens. Over the generations they'd intermarried until it was just one big, miserable clan. Not legal incest, understand, but near enough so the sickness took hold. The Bonners had this ramshackle homestead on the east side of the creek, and the Cullens were on the west side, right opposite. Folks used to joke about them having beds that floated across to the other side. Between the two shacks there were ten or twelve adults and their various common-law wives and husbands and God knows how many children running loose. The adult population fluctuated, depending on who was in prison that year, you understand?"

"I think I'm beginning to," I said.

"Both clans lived off the swamp, poaching mostly, and whatever they could steal. There was a game warden got shot, no one could narrow it down further than it had to be a Bonner or a Cullen. Never made an arrest for that murder, but two or three of the men were always in jail or out on bail or contesting charges for theft, assault, rape, you name it. Except nobody ever tried to put them away for the worst crime of all, and that was what was being done to the children. Used to make my skin crawl. You could see it in the kids' eyes, the sickness that was being inflicted on them. You get fifteen or twenty people sleeping in one room, most of them drunk or half-crazy or retarded, and ugly stuff happens, usually to the children."

"Nobody from the state tried to intervene?"

Irene sighed. "You'd have had to have been there. These were dangerous, violent people. Scary people. Still are, because I'm sure nothing much has changed except they're working on a new generation or two.

A social worker would have to go in there with a Sherman tank, if he wanted to come out alive."

"I assume we're getting around to Jake Bonner?"

She shuddered, as if the name itself caused pain. "It's hard," she said. "That boy has been clawing at the inside of me ever since Mary Beth first brought him home. She was seventeen, and willful. Not afraid of anything or anyone. Full of beans, Pete liked to say. Being a father, he was partially blind to what was going on with Mary Beth. I knew better. Once or twice when we went to the islands for holidays, I'd had my hands full keeping her out of trouble. Anyhow, Jake was a handsome boy. Had an 'outside momma,' which was swamp talk for saying his mother wasn't a blood relative of either clan. Poor thing was from Fort Myers, and she got herself mixed up with a couple of different Bonners. No one really knew who sired Jake, or any of those kids, for that matter. He must have inherited his mother's brains, though, because he was about twice as smart as any of his kin. A year or two before Mary Beth got stuck on him, his mama drowned herself in the swamp. That was how they ruled it. Most of the folks in Indigo figured she might have had a little help."

"Any suspects?"

"Take your pick. The men were all mean sober and worse drunk."

"Jake inherit anything?"

That got me a funny look. "Not much, I wouldn't think. Maybe enough to buy new clothes and a pair of shoes. Like I say, he was a good-looking boy. He was smart and he knew what he wanted. Mary Beth thought he wanted her, but I knew right away what he really wanted was what Mary Beth represented: money, success, a way out of Indigo Springs. I tried to talk sense into her, and so did Pete, but she was seventeen and she was in love, and that was that. So what happened, finally, Mary Beth and Jake ran off the day she graduated from high school. We had a big party all set for her, and this little car Pete wanted to give her, and she just never came back home."

They heard from Mary Beth now and then, starting a few weeks after she eloped. Usually in the form of a late-night telephone call.

"It's funny how close you can feel to a child when she's growing up. Until she got mixed up with Jake Bonner, Mary Beth used to tell me everything. Then she didn't tell me anything. I didn't even know she was pregnant until she had the baby, and then I realized she must have been pregnant before they run off. Didn't know where they lived, exactly. Pete found out, though, once the baby was born, and we went over there to Fort Lauderdale and tried to patch things up. They were doing okay—Jake was managing a club and he tried to talk Pete into going into the bar business. Pete wouldn't have anything to do with it, but he did give them some money—a few thousand to pay off the hospital bills.

"So that was how it stood, once Penny was born. I wasn't going to let anything get in the way of seeing our granddaughter, so we just smiled and nodded and put up with the situation. The situation being that Jake Bonner was—is—a smart-mouth phony. I suppose we'd have continued along that way, visiting on holidays and making special trips to see the baby, only Pete decided to give Mary Beth a special birthday present."

What happened was that Pete Broscoe had finally decided to cut himself loose from Indigo Springs and from the construction business. He'd ridden the boom up and had the foresight to see the bottom of the cycle was going to come through and bump him off if he didn't diversify into a less turbulent business. He went ahead and sold his company and his various land investments and bought a place on Marco Island.

"The idea was, we'd get a boat and just play for a couple of years. Take our retirement early. And then, when Pete got bored with the soft life, he'd get himself back into business. Well, he bought the house and the boat, and the other thing he did was set up his finances to take care of me and Mary Beth. Some of the cash he put into trusts. A half-million for me, and a hundred thousand for Mary Beth. Set up to pay quarterly dividends. For her birthday that year he turned over the first dividend check. I think it was about two thousand. Not a lot, but he figured the extra income would come in handy for a young couple. Also, although he never told Mary Beth, we thought it would be good if she had a little income of her own, in case she ever wanted to cut loose from Jake."

Irene was convinced that in signing over that first dividend check her husband had been signing his own death warrant.

"A month or later Pete got a call. This was about ten at night. Someone down at the marina calling to say the lines on his boat had come loose and the hull was banging up against the pilings. Pete gave me a kiss and walked out the door, and that's the last time I saw him alive."

Pete Broscoe had come to a peculiar end. Peculiar but not unfamiliar—at least not to me. Somehow or other he'd got himself tangled in the lines to his boat, fallen overboard, and drowned.

"So Mary Beth got the trust and she gave it to Jake, and that's what he'd wanted all along."

"And you think Jake was responsible for your husband's death?"

She nodded fervently. "You bet I do. Pete was the carefulest man you ever saw around a boat. Meticulous about every detail. No way he would get a coil of rope wrapped around his ankles, arm, and neck, and then fall over. Somebody wrapped him up and pushed him in the water and watched him drown. It wasn't Jake himself—he's too smart for that. He was tending bar that night and had a couple of hundred alibis. Had to be kin of his. A Bonner or a Cullen."

Or maybe a pair of Cullens. Who had the old rope trick perfected by the time they got around to Bert Hamper.

"Was there an inquest, Mrs. Broscoe?"

"Yes, there was an inquest. I wasn't the only one who thought that Pete's death was just too damn convenient. The county sheriff put his homicide detective onto it, but he couldn't develop any evidence. He came out here holding his hat in his hand and told me that, like it or not, there were people in this world who got away with murder. Said it happened regularly."

The sheriff was an honest man, even if he hadn't been much of a detective. Murder-for-hire was gotten away with on a basis so regular that conviction for the crime was the exception, not the rule.

"What about Mary Beth?" I said. "Was she in on it?"

"No way," Irene said, shaking her head vigorously. "I'm positive she wasn't. Mary Beth was never on-purpose hurtful. And she was always blind to the bad in Jake. Just could not believe he'd do anything so wrong and evil as have her father murdered so he could get his hands on the money. We had a terrible row about it, and that was when Jake got an unlisted phone, so he wouldn't have to listen to me telling him I *knew* what he was even if Mary Beth didn't."

Irene Broscoe had not gone easy into her good night. She had raged at Jake Bonner, raged at him over the telephone and on his doorstep, until he had gotten a court injunction forbidding her calls or visits. The injunction had extended to visits with her grandchild, who was two years old at the time the court order went into effect.

"A few times Mary Beth snuck away and let me see the child. Then Jake put a stop to that, too."

"But you called Penny on her birthday?"

"What Mary Beth would sometimes do, for special days like birthdays and Christmas, is call me and let me talk to Penny for a few minutes. Jake didn't like that one bit. Told Mary Beth I would try to poison the girl's heart. Which I never did. I only wanted to tell her I loved her and wish her a Merry Christmas or a Happy Birthday or whatever."

The small black gull was persistent. It swooped and dived, harassing the flock of larger birds. Finally it managed to snatch a fish right out of the beak of a careless pelican.

"The one thing I never thought would happen," Irene said, staring at the green sea. "The one thing I never ever imagined is that the murderous, manipulative son of a bitch would kill my little girl. My Mary Beth. She was too valuable to him. In the name of God, if he was tired of her, why didn't he just divorce her?"

She looked at me as if I might actually have the answer. "I don't know what happened, Mrs. Broscoe. But it seems like every time Jake Bonner needs money or is threatened, someone dies. It's a habit with him, and so far he's gotten away with it."

"Know what?" Irene said. "Know how I found out about Mary Beth dying? I read it in the paper, way on the back pages. By then it was old news. I had to call every funeral home in Coral Gables before I could find out where she was buried. I went down there, and do you know he hadn't even put a proper stone on her grave? Just a temporary marker. I paid for the monument myself. And then I went straight to the police and I told them my daughter had sure as hell been murdered. Jake must have pushed her under that poor girl's car. The police were very nice to me, but I could tell they thought I was crazy with grief. An important man like Jake Bonner wouldn't murder his wife. But that's what he did. He waited until the last second and then he pushed Mary Beth in the way of that car."

It dawned on me that Irene Broscoe, isolated and bitter in her Marco Island solitude, had missed the marriage notice in the *Herald*, or failed to put the two names together.

"You know that Jake remarried?" I said.

"I heard. The bastard didn't wait long, did he? I feel sorry for the poor woman who married him, whoever she is."

"Her name is Lee Ann Chambers, Mrs. Broscoe, or that's the name she was using at the time. From what you've told me I think maybe the Chambers part is a recent invention. Because it was Lee Ann who was driving the car that killed your daughter.

And Jake hired two of her relatives to handle his security and do his dirty work."

"No," Irene said, covering her face. "It's not possible."

"Ellis and Orrin Cullen, Mrs. Broscoe, that's who Jake put on the payroll. Kin of Lee Ann's, Penny told me. Which also means they may be kin of her father's. And you know what that means."

Irene stood up. Her face was ashen. "I'm going to be sick," she announced.

I held her as she knelt in the white sand. And when she was finished being sick, she asked me if I would help her find a way to kill Jake Bonner.

17

THE plan was simple. Irene would stay in the hotel suite and get acquainted with her granddaughter. That would take some time, as they were both frightened by the prospect, Irene more so than Penny. Mutt would stay with them as lookout and guardian while I went off to take a poke at Jake Bonner.

Not to kill him, mind you. I didn't do murders for hire, no matter how just the motive, sweet the revenge, or deserving the victim. Moral reservations aside, Florida had reinstated the death penalty, and the governor wasn't afraid of expending electricity to carry it out.

The poke I had in mind would cause Jake to panic and behave in such a way as to interest the relevant authorities in reopening the investigations of several "accidental" deaths—including the murder by arson of Connie Geiger. The main arrow in my quiver was the almost certain knowledge that despite her convincing tale about love at first sight, Lee Ann and Jake had been acquainted before Mary Beth's death. That in fact they were, at the very least, cousins.

Kissing cousins.

That was what Penny had been trying to tell me, with her uneasy references to the "family stuff" she had overheard just prior to running away. No one appreciates the power of a lie better than a child who has been lied to, and Penny instinctively knew that if Jake and Lee Ann were lying about their past, then it followed that her mother's death was a lie, too.

Proving it was another thing. I needed hard evidence. Going back to the source seemed like the right idea. It wasn't, but how was a guy to know?

I cut across the state twice that day. No, three times, although the last was purely unintended. The first crossing took me east along the Tamiami to the Florida Turnpike and then a few exits north to Fort Lauderdale. I stopped at a mush-burger franchise and waited for a teenage girl to give up the pay phone. It was like waiting for rain in Death Valley.

My patience expired before the conversation did.

"I don't want to use the phone," I said, "at least not until it's been disinfected. I do want to look at the Yellow Pages."

"Get outta here, you geek, I'll scream."

"Go ahead," I said. "Just don't choke on your bubble gum. Now let me get at the phone book. It's an emergency."

I tore the book from the rack. Temper, temper, T.D. You don't want to get arrested, not yet. I flipped through the book, looking for the listings of radio stations. The teenager was making squawking noises, working herself up to a full-blown scream. I decided to tear the page out and leave the scene of the crime.

The WPIX studio was situated in a shopping center on Broward Boulevard. The shopping center had fallen on hard times, and the original chains and franchises had abandoned their storefronts to the usual pet shops, discount retailers, beauty schools, and chiropractors that move in like second growth after a forest fire. One of the bigger spaces was occupied by something advertising itself as the Pixton College of Broadcasting.

The studio for the school radio station was highly visible behind a plate-glass wall. A jagged crack ran through the glass, held together by a ragged strip of silver duct tape. If the studio was a form of advertising for the school, the cracked glass was the truth-in-lending clause. Electronic drum noises blasted from outside speakers. I happen to enjoy rock music, so long as it contains an element of music. I draw the line at unaccompanied electronic drum noises. I guess that means I'm getting old. That and the fact that I've never been tempted to shave off my hair, or dye it.

A young lady with a partially scalped head occupied the stool at the transmitting console. She was engaged in a spirited telephone conversation. I wondered if she was talking to the teenager I'd offended at the mush-burger franchise. Anything is possible in Lauderdale, as party animals everywhere will testify. I waved through the glass. The girl smirked and waved back. I decided right then that I wasn't in the mood to converse with anyone who shaved part of her head and dyed the rest electric pink and played drum noise at peak volume.

I veered to the left and entered the "college" reception area. The electro drums boomed inside, too. It was everywhere, like air pollution. I covered my ears while approaching the counter. The male clerk had hair the same shade of pink. There was no escape. He did, however, consent to lowering the volume.

"Remember Ginger Baker?" I said.

"Ginger who?"

149

"Before you were born," I said. "Long boring drum solos, but they didn't hurt. Looked like he'd been soaking in a vat of Methedrine."

"What?"

"Ginger Baker. Never mind. Why I'm here, I'm trying to locate a dj who used to work for 'PIX. Lee Ann Chambers."

The welcoming smile vanished, just like that.

"We can't give out information about former students."

"She was a dj. Pretty, blond, sexy voice."

"Yeah," Mr. Pink said, avoiding my eyes. "All the dj's are students. They take the courses, get airtime, pass the FCC exam, and move on."

I propped my elbows against the counter and tried to look nonthreatening. I was interested in why he had reacted so instantly to the name "Lee Ann Chambers." I checked out the nameplate and said, "Alvin, has anyone attempted to bribe you in the last six months or so?"

"You'll have to leave now," he said. "I'm very busy."

I reached in my pocket and came out with a wad of the bills I'd scooped from Penny's backpack. I liked the idea of spending Jake Bonner's money.

"Here's a hundred for lowering the drums. Here's another hundred because you stopped smiling. Here's another hundred because Alvin is a nice honest name. Here's another hundred because—"

"Stop!" he said, pushing my hand away. "Why are you *doing* this?"

"Because I'm in a hurry," I said, letting the bills flutter to the desk. "Because I don't have the time to go get a cop and get the cop to get the warrant and present the warrant and check out your files. I could tell you that a little girl's life depends on it, but you probably wouldn't believe me, would you?"

"No," he said, staring at the little pile of bills. Usually looking at money makes people happy. It made Alvin sad.

"All you have to do is look in Lee Ann Chambers' file and tell me what her real name is and where she's from."

"I can't."

"Here's another hundred because you should never say can't. Remember the little choo-choo train? I *can* I *can* I *know* I can."

Alvin tossed the money with his fingers. Fluffing it into shape, like he was making a salad. "File's gone," he sighed.

"Ah-ha," I said. "Hence the eclipsed smile at the mention of her name."

Alvin raised his pink eyebrows. "You sure talk funny, mister. The reason I can't take the money is because I already sold the file on Lee Ann Chambers."

"Do tell," I said. "You remember who you sold it to, by any chance?"

He shook his head. "Some insurance investigator. That's what he said, anyway. I figured he was from a collection agency. The collection-agency creeps come in here all the time, checking out the student-loan defaulters. I never ask their names."

"Bert Hamper," I said.

"Who?"

"Fan of Frank Sinatra. Never mind who Frank is, I haven't got time to explain. Look, maybe you can still help. I don't need the whole file. Her original application would do."

Alvin stopped fluffing the money and perked up. He went to the row of file cabinets and let his fingers do the walking. He frowned, shook his head, walked a little farther through the file, and returned fluttering a sheet of paper.

"This is the inquiry questionnaire, not the formal application. I doubt the address is current."

He handed me the questionnaire. It looked like something a playmate of the month had to fill out to complete the centerfold, but it had all the information I needed to get the T. D. Stash Talent Show back on the road.

> Name: Lee Ann Chambers
> Address: General Delivery,
> Indigo Springs, FL

I skipped the stuff about career goals. I had a pretty good idea what career Lee Ann had in mind.

18

"HI-HO, hi-ho, it's up the creek we go."

Don't blame me for singing. It was Mutt's fault; he'd neglected to specify a tape deck when he rented the car, and the only relief from the monotonous drive to Indigo Springs—"Go up the creek," Irene had said, "and keep on going"—was to see if I could hit as many bad notes as there were ruts in the road.

Around me the Big Cypress was beginning to take form. Not that there are many giant cypress left. Most of the big trees were logged out years ago, used to make pickle barrels and coffins. During epidemics the former were used in place of the latter, if you can believe the old-timers. Some of the big trees were simply chopped and left to rot in the muck by swamp men protesting the intrusion of government regulation. What's left are the dwarf cypress, impressive in their own way, drenched with moss and strangler fig.

Hundreds of small waterways penetrate the swamp, and the Indigo Creek was one or sometimes two of them, it was hard to tell. The road followed roughly in the same northeasterly direction. Now and then the creek would be lost to view, vanishing behind slash pines and cypress hammocks, or widening into a slough. Eventually it began to deepen, holding its shape. I began to pass ramshackle homesteads. When I came upon a hound dog sleeping serenely in the road, I took it as a sign that civilization—or the Big Cypress version of it, anyhow—could not be far off.

Indigo Springs was all Irene Broscoe had promised, and less. She hadn't mentioned the six-store shopping mall, of which half the outlets were boarded up and the remaining three competed in the renting of adult videos. Nor had she bothered to tell me that the library, the municipal office, the fire department, and the post office were all located under the same rusty tin roof.

All four town offices were represented in the person of Mrs. Roland G. Pew. That was according to the nameplate above the little cage containing the postal facilities. Mrs. Pew smoked small black cigars. She was slightly bigger than your average fire hydrant, and better-looking, if you like blue hair and costume jewelry. She was a character of the type found only in the most remote and godforsaken spots, and since I have a weakness for characters, I decided to trust her.

My mistake.

I had my opening gambit ready. "Mrs. Pew, I'm visiting the lovely town of Indigo Springs as a researcher for the Greater Miami Talent Showcase. I wonder if I might prevail upon you for a few snippets of information."

"I ain't wearin' no nekkid bathing suit," she said, setting things straight right off the bat. "Mr. Pew don't approve."

On the way out of Lauderdale I'd bought a *guayabera* with a lot of cheap, fancy stitchwork. I had borrowed Mutt's new panama hat. I was the height of fashion in Indigo Springs, the traveling drummer irresistible to backwoods maidens and blue-haired ladies. Or so I hoped.

I gave her my best smile and said, "Then Mr. Pew is a man of rare distinction. I entirely agree. We don't have our contestants parade around in sinful attire, Mrs. Pew. No, indeed! We in the Greater Miami Talent Showcase believe in upholding standards of decorum. Which is precisely what I'm doing here in lovely Indigo Springs."

Mrs. Pew puffed on her cigar and regarded me with open suspicion. She got off her stool and came out of the post-office cage, assuming, with that subtle change of location, the office of town clerk.

"T'ain't hardly a lovely place, young man. Now whyn't you stop talkin' ragtime and tell me what you after?"

"Background investigation, Mrs. Pew. We have to check out each and every contestant. Make sure they're as upright and proper as can be. Most of the girls are just squeaky clean, but now and again the bad apple gets in the barrel, if you know what I mean."

"Mmmm," Mrs. Pew said, indicating the affirmative. Her cigar, from the subtle scent, was rum-soaked. "Who's the victim?"

"Pardon me?"

"Who you all checkin' out, sugar? Give me a name. And don't suppose I can waste my time for no recompense, neither."

Ah, now we were getting down to business. I slipped a carefully folded bill out of a *guayabera* pocket. Mrs. Pew caught a glimpse of Ulysses S. Grant and surrendered. She didn't have as many opportunities to supplement her income as Alvin the college receptionist, but she wasn't about to pass up the chance.

"The lady in question calls herself Lee Ann Chambers," I said.

Mrs. Pew sucked deeply on the black cigar as she ran her thumb down the list of the town census.

"No Chambers here. Not a one."

"The last name may have been assumed. I can maybe save us both some time. Is the librarian in?"

Mrs. Pew got up from the town clerk's desk and crossed to the back corner of the building, where all eight shelves of the Indigo Springs Public Library were located.

"On duty," she said. "Hurry it along, sugar, the meter's runnin'."

"High-school yearbooks?"

She nodded and pointed to the shelf. "Not many here as bothers with high school after the minimum."

I was counting on Lee Ann. She was ambitious and beautiful and she'd managed to get out of Indigo Springs. The type of attractive, confident girl who would make an impression in high school, even if she didn't stick it out long enough to graduate.

I found her, appropriately enough, under cheerleaders. With the little skirt and the long legs and the blond ponytail and the pom-poms. Anna Lee Cullen. I turned to the bios and found her again. Anna L. Cullen *Nickname:* Annie; *Honors:* Typing Certificate; *Activities:* Glee Club, Varsity Cheerleader, Media Club; *Goal in Life:* A career in broadcasting.

A ring of smoke drifted into my field of vision. When I turned around Mrs. Pew was walking back to the town-clerk desk, her curiosity satisfied. I thumbed through the book, found no other useful entries, and asked the town clerk if there was by any chance a photocopy machine on the premises. There was, in the post office.

"Under the wanted posters," she said.

It was the kind of irony best appreciated when you're wearing a panama hat. I made a copy of Anna Lee in her cheerleading outfit. The reproduction was bad, but no worse than the rest of the wanted posters. I was dutifully returning the yearbook to the shelf when I noticed Mrs. Pew hanging up the phone.

"That's funny," I said. "I didn't hear it ring."

"Family business," she said, hiding behind a pall of cigar smoke.

There was a screech of brakes, not far away. I looked out the window and saw a black El Camino pickup truck at the curb. A big guy got out of the cab. Then another big guy got out of the cab. The second big guy had his left arm in a sling. He was clean-shaven, which revealed an amazing lack of chin, considering his size and girth. The first big guy had a funny-looking beard. Like maybe it had been singed in a fire.

I said, "Mrs. Pew, I am *very* disappointed."

It all boiled down to a question of getting from Point A to Point B. Point A was the Indigo Springs municipal building. Point B was the front seat of the rented car, under which I'd stashed a Smith & Wesson .38 revolver. The very same firearm that had set off the explosion that had failed, obviously, to do any lasting harm to those two lovable twins, Ellis and Orrin Cullen.

The bad-news brothers, home for a brief convalescence. Probably a little irritated, if the deer rifles and the buck knives were any indication. Interested in checking out the stranger who was checking out Anna Lee.

I turned the lock on the front door.

"Keep your head down, Mrs. Pew."

Mrs. Pew had retreated to the post office. Maybe she intended to check the posters and see if I was considered armed and dangerous. I pushed her town-clerk desk against the door. The knob rattled. There was a curse and then boots began to connect, heavily, with the door panels.

Mrs. Pew decided to get down on the floor. The floor was tempting, but I had my heart set on a rear exit. Getting to Point B, that seemed very important.

What I did was go out through the bathroom window. The time-honored egress of check bouncers, gumshoes, and visiting boyfriends. I left part of the *guayabera* on the windowsill. Never did know what happened to Mutt's new hat. Maybe the brothers ate it. They were mad enough to, by the time we had again exchanged greetings.

The first Cullen I ran into was the one with his arm in a sling. I came around the corner going flat out and we collided. The rifle went flying. The arm must have been tender, because Ellis or Orrin or whoever he was, he screamed. Like a girl. I guess it was more of a shriek. He got to his knees, cradling the arm to his body. I could see where he'd cut himself shaving, which must have been tough to do with only his left hand functioning.

There's an old saying, never kick a man when he's down. Never made sense to me. Kicking a man when he's up is rarely effective. So I picked up the deer rifle and kicked him in his bad arm, just as hard as I could, and what do you know, he fainted! Passed out like a sophomore at a keg party, with an I-drank-the-whole-thing pallor making a gray mask of his face.

Meanwhile, back at the bathroom window, twin brother had got himself stuck. He had one big shoulder through and had discovered there just wasn't room for the other shoulder and his thick neck, too. Seeing me with his brother's rifle in my hands inspired a paroxysm of wiggling. He assumed that I was going to do what he would have done in my place, and that was shoot point-blank.

In retrospect, it would have been a wise move. Instead of shooting, however, I took hold of the rifle barrel and swung for the bleachers. He saw it coming and tried to shift his head out of the way, but it was hard to miss anything that ugly. The sound of what happened when the rifle butt connected sickened me almost as much as it sickened him. I take that back. He felt much worse.

The brother with the bad flipper was still out cold. Never even moved when I slipped the buck knife out his belt.

Mrs. Pew was standing in the ruptured doorway when I came around to the front of the building. Surprised to see me. Well, I was surprised to be there. The keys were in the ignition of the El Camino. I pocketed them and then used the buck knife to deflate all four tires.

Better safe than sorry, that's my motto.

19

SOMEWHERE around Ochopee the shakes hit me. Bad enough so I had to pull over and get out of the car. There was a puddle of icewater in my belly and my knees had come unhinged somehow. The after-shock of adrenaline and fear. There were a couple of elderly black men fishing in the canal that runs along the Tamiami Trail and they had along a cooler full of beer. I asked if I could buy a can and they said absolutely not, that they were too well along in years to go into a new business and that therefore if I wanted a beer I would have to accept one for free. Or two, if I had the need.

"One will do," I said.

"You look like you seen a ghost, Mr. Man."

"A couple of ghosts," I said.

The beer helped. A few miles down the trail I stopped at a tourist trap and ate something euphemistically referred to as a Dixie Deluxe Cheeseburger. If you're tough enough to down one of those babies, you're tough enough to take on a smooth-talking blonde whose goal in life was a career in broadcasting.

On my way out the door I cashed in a few bills and took the change to the pay phone outside. First call was to the Marco Beach Hotel & Villa, where Mutt reported that everything was copacetic. Irene and Penny were playing Chinese checkers—Mutt had been playing, too, but then he'd lost his marbles. Later he planned on picking up takeout food as a change from the hotel room-service fare.

It sounded like a picture of domestic tranquillity.

"How's by you, bubba?" Mutt wanted to know.

"Going like clockwork," I said.

"You sound a little funny."

"I think I just ate a microwaved woodchuck."

"Yum-yum," Mutt said. "So, how long do you think this operation is going to take?"

"A few days. Think you can stand it?"

He chuckled. "Sharing a luxury suite with a beautiful widow ain't exactly doing hard time, bubba."

Hanging up, I tried to picture Mutt Durgin romantically involved with Irene Broscoe. Stranger things had happened, although I couldn't think of any right off.

My next call was to the *Miami Herald*, Financial Desk.

"Stanley Horn," he said, wheezing slightly.

"Stan the man," I said. "You think a Pulitzer might cure that asthma?"

"Stash? Jesus, don't hang up. I thought you were dead."

"Why would you think a thing like that?"

" 'Cause I've been putting a few things together on your friend Shake'n Jake and I am now convinced that getting in his way has proved to be a lethal mistake for at least three people. Also, he reported that his boat was stolen and later destroyed in the Everglades. I thought you might have been on it."

I told him, briefly, how the lovely Rybovich sport-fishing machine had met its end.

"Wow," he said. "Hey, this is great stuff."

"Not for publication, it isn't," I said. "At least not for a few more days. Are you going to write the story?"

"We had a meeting just this morning. The *Herald* doesn't get into something like this lightly, you know. The subject and sources have to be vetted by the legal department. But now that the FBI has indicated, off the record, that Bonner is under investigation, the decision has been made to go ahead with a spotlight series. In depth and thoroughly researched. Which means our investigative team will get first crack. That leaves me with the primary source."

"Primary source?"

"You," Horn said. "I get to write about you. Your version. Small-time fishing guide takes on big-time businessman. Brawn versus brain."

"Thanks," I said.

"Hey, if you want we'll work out a different angle. What I need to know now is, when and where do you plan to give yourself up?"

I said, "I dunno, Stan. How about New Year's Eve, in Times Square?"

He said, "Don't hang up!"

I hung up and dialed a more familiar number. Lily Cashman's male secretary answered and informed me that Ms. Cashman was with a client.

"Try interrupting, Richard. She'll respect you for it."

"Is this T.D.? Oh, my gosh, I'm *sure* she wants to talk to you."

What Lil wanted to do was lecture me. I was a stubborn, careless fool with no respect for my own safety or the concern of my dearest friends. I had no business taking the law into my own hands, and if I was going to continue to behave that way, I could be damned sure Lil Cashman wasn't going to put her reputation on the line for me, or risk disbarment on my behalf.

When she paused for breath, I said, "I love you, too, Lil."

"You had us scared to death, T.D. I'll take back everything I just said if you'll come back home and let me handle everything through the proper channels. I can get most of the charges dismissed, I think."

Everybody wanted me to turn myself in. It was the latest fad.

"Lil, I've heard rumors about the FBI deciding to investigate Jake Bonner. Any truth?"

"The word is they suspect that Bonner faked a ransom note that was supposedly from you. Then they got a tip that an insurance investigator had died under mysterious circumstances and they're checking out that angle and how it might bear on his wife's death."

No doubt the tipster had an asthmatic wheeze.

"Where does that leave me?"

Lil hemmed and hawed. I told her to give it to me straight, no beating around the palm tree.

"There will be charges," she admitted. "All bailable. All you'd have to do is agree to turn the girl over to the court. We could probably get an injunction preventing return to her father's custody."

"Probably?"

"You wanted it straight, lover. So far Bonner hasn't been charged with any crimes. You have."

"And if he is charged?"

"That changes things. How much I can't say. Jake Bonner isn't exactly the only South Florida businessman who's under investigation by an agency of the federal government. He'd have plenty of company at any country club in Dade County. He'll do what rich men always do when threatened by justice: hire a ball-busting law firm."

"I'm shocked," I said. "You mean that money has an undue influence on truth, justice, and the American way?"

Leave 'em laughing, that's another one of my mottoes.

The Haitians were still landed in Coral Gables. Raking the marble chips, clipping the grass, scrubbing the white stucco. Moving like silent, black wraiths through the sun-bleached landscape. The latest thing in slave labor. Their manacles were invisible, but no less real. Without green cards or visas the choice was limited. Work for subminimum wages or be deported.

Give us your poor, your huddled masses yearning to work cheap.

I parked in the driveway and went right up to the front entrance and rang the bell. Either the FBI had the place staked out or they didn't. If they did, my little plan was a loser, and I might as well surrender to the gentlemen in the gray suits.

Marita answered the door. As before, her face was an expressionless black mask. There was no spark of recognition in her eyes. I was just another white man, a potential threat to her well-being.

"Lady of the house at home?" I asked. "I'm here to demonstrate the world's smallest vacuum cleaner. I've got it right here in my pocket."

She glanced down, noted the bulge in my pocket, did not react except to say, "Missy don't see nobody."

"Give her this." I handed her the paper airplane

I'd made out of the photocopy from the yearbook. Anna Lee Cullen, this is your life, airmail and special delivery.

I could have just barged right in, but the idea was to set a tone of civility. We were going to be reasonable. We were going to negotiate.

After a few minutes Marita returned and nodded. I followed her to the enclosed veranda. As Yogi Berra would have said, it was déjà vu all over again, except that this time the current Mrs. Bonner was dressed all in white. White Spandex tights, a white silk blouse, pearl earrings, pale lipstick. She was standing at the bar, pouring Russian vodka over ice. The paper airplane was on the tiled floor. It looked like maybe she'd stepped on it.

The pale-blue, almond-shaped eyes were as cool as the chips of ice in the drink she handed me.

"I could have you arrested. Just like that."

"You're on the wrong page, Annie. You're supposed to say 'Where's Penny? Is my darling stepdaughter okay?' "

She swirled the ice in her glass, made up her mind about something, and then sat down in a wicker chair, facing me. I sat down, too, and made myself comfy. The .38 was pinching my thigh, so I took it out and put it on the arm of the chair, next to the drink. Lee Ann looked at it and smiled. Nobody in the Bonner household was taking my firepower seriously.

"Penny is wrong about us," she said. "She's just a mixed-up kid. She jumped to conclusions."

"Tell you what, Annie. You tell me what you want me to believe and I'll listen politely and then outline a way that just might possibly keep you out of prison. Off death row, anyhow."

She chuckled and shook her head. Death row, prison, what a preposterous idea *that* was.

"I'll tell you the truth," she said. "Then you can apologize for causing us so much trouble and maybe *you'll* stay out of jail."

"I'm listening, Annie."

She settled herself into the chair, tucking her bare feet under her bottom, and sipped the vodka. Her bemused expression was disconcerting, to say the least. I'd been expecting anger, or cunning, or outright denial. Not bemused interest in setting me straight.

"Okay," she said, "first things first. You found out I changed my name. It's true, I did change it, mostly for professional reasons. I wanted to get into radio or TV and Annie Cullen sounded kind of, I don't know, frumpy, so I came up with Lee Ann Chambers. I made it official in court. It's not like I was trying to hide anything."

I took a sip of the drink and was reminded that I didn't much like vodka. "The name change is no big deal. The big deal is you told the cops that you and Jake had never met prior to the accident. And you gave me that beautiful, phony story about falling in love at the inquest. When the truth is you grew up right across the creek from each other."

Lee Ann smiled prettily. She shook her head, a little disappointed in me. "Give me a chance, huh? I was about to say the second thing is about Jake and me. If you've been to Indigo Springs, you already know my family and his are real close. Swamp kin, they call it. Just plain old white trash is what we were. He got out when I was twelve or thirteen. Run off with the one and only rich girl in town. I got to admit, it put ideas in my head. Only thing, there weren't any rich boys to run off with. So what I did, I determined to wash the swamp off me somehow and then run off alone, if need be."

"It's almost perfect," I said, acknowledging her sophisticated poise, her "look." "Must have been hard to drop that accent, though. Jake never quite managed it."

Lee Ann nodded, touching her ear, caressing the lobe. "I listened to the radio and the TV, so I could be like the people I saw there. I listened and I watched and I learned. Then I took elocution in the regional high school and a lot of courses at this broadcasting school up in Lauderdale. That's how I happened to see Jake again. 'Course I knew he'd made it big, and the fact that he had a chain of discos gave me a good excuse to call on him. Looking for a dj job. Not that he owed me anything in particular. We came from the same part of the swamp, is all. Anyhow, Jake could hardly believe it was me. 'You that little skinny thing with the towhead and the buck teeth?' Like that. Anyhow, he sort of promised me a job, whenever there was an opening. And then we had a few drinks and talked about old times. I never meant to get involved with him. It was sort of accidental. It was, you know, at first it was just this physical thing." She paused. "Something wrong with the drink?"

I said, "I'm not thirsty."

"Honey, you want to relax, okay?" Lee Ann pulled her chair closer. She placed a warm hand over my knee and gently squeezed. "I really and truly think we can work out this problem, once you hear my side of the story."

"Yup," I said, clearing my throat. "You were telling me about Jake."

"I was, wasn't I? I guess we don't want to get distracted, do we?"

"No," I said, trying to sound convincing.

"Well, then, what happened with Jake and me is that it just *happened*. I never in a million years figured I'd end up married to the guy. I mean, he was still in love with his wife and that was fine by me. He didn't want to hurt Mary Beth. What we had was different. This intense physical thing, you know?"

I believed her about the intense physical thing. I believed it even more when she leaned closer and lowered her voice to a husky whisper and said, "I have these needs, honey."

"Needs" is not an erotically charged word, ordinarily. It was the way Lee Ann used it.

"I get these impulses," she said.

It was amazing what she could do with ordinary words like "need" and "impulse."

"That's what Jake and I had. Great sex. I mean really great. But he wasn't going to leave Mary Beth and I didn't want him to. Honest."

"No?" I said. It wasn't much of a question, but I was having a little problem with my concentration.

"Just a fling," she said, letting her fingers play a few slow chords on my thigh. "Just an impulse, that's all it was."

I inched my chair back. It was showing weakness, maybe, but it was necessary to put some distance between us.

"But you did marry him," I said. "After you ran over his first wife."

"That was just one of those awful coincidences. It happened exactly like I told the police and you and everybody else. It was dark, the car was unfamiliar. I thought I had the headlight on, but probably I didn't. I didn't even know it was Jake and Mary Beth coming through the parking lot. Anyhow, Mary Beth didn't see me or she stumbled, I don't know which. I never even knew she was there until after."

"Maybe she didn't stumble," I said. "Maybe she was pushed."

Lee Ann shook her head firmly. I was wrong, dead wrong. "No way, honey. Jake would never do a thing like that. He loved Mary Beth. But we knew no one would believe us, even though it really and truly was an accident. Mary Beth was dead, God rest her, and it wouldn't make any difference to her what we said. So we made up the fib about not knowing each other, and now it's gotten all turned around somehow."

I said, "It's not going to work. You tell it real nice, Lee Ann, but it's not going to work."

She gave me that sorrowful little headshake she'd perfected. How could I be so stubborn as to not believe her?

"You want to know how come we got married after all, if we hadn't been in love before," she said. "That's the part you're doubtful on."

"One of several."

"I just don't know why it's so hard to believe that love happens. Jake was all alone and it was my fault, and he seemed so protective of that little girl. It was just so sweet, to see how sorrowful they were. And so my heart melted. I wanted to make it up, like I told you before, I wanted to be a mother to that poor little girl."

"Penny," I said.

"I do know her name."

I said, "Lee Ann, even if Mary Beth's death was just an 'awful coincidence,' as you put it, it doesn't stop there. Someone is killing people. Someone killed Mary Beth's father and succeeded in making it look like an accident. Someone killed an insurance investigator named Bert Hamper, using the same 'accident.' Someone tried to kill Penny in Key West and *did* kill an innocent bystander. Two someones tried to kill Penny and me in the Everglades, and no doubt will try again, if given the chance."

Lee Ann smiled and shook her head. I kept disappointing her. "That's a lot of silly talk, honey. No one wants to kill Penny. That's something she made up after she heard her dad and me talking about the old days in Indigo Springs."

"Ellis and Orrin," I said. "They followed me back to Key West and set a house afire. Then they tracked us into the Everglades. Shooting real bullets from real guns, Lee Ann. Shooting to kill."

"I don't believe it. Not those two sweet boys."

"They do the killing for Jake, Lee Ann. I think it started with Mary Beth's father. Jake wanted him dead, and the twins obliged. They've been holding that over him ever since. Now they've got you married to him, and that makes the clan connection even tighter. But it doesn't really change anything, Lee Ann, and it doesn't get Jake off the hook. In Florida he can still get the chair, even if he didn't tie the ropes or light the fires or pull the trigger. And you can go down, too. You're part of it."

Lee Ann said, "I don't know anything about any killings. You're making this up. It's a lie."

I stood up and slipped the .38 into my waistband. "There's only one way you can play this, Lee Ann. Go to the cops with me and agree to testify against Jake. If you do it voluntarily, maybe a jury will believe you're an innocent bystander."

170

Lee Ann slipped out of the chair and came to me. She placed her hands on my chest and began to stroke the delicate spot over my heart.

"I am innocent," she whispered huskily. "I can prove it."

I should have stopped it right then. I should have backed up and pulled out the gun and said something, anything, to make it stop. Instead, I let her keep touching me and all I could think to say was, "How?"

She put her lips to my ear and murmured, "I've got proof. Hidden away where it's safe."

"Where's that, Lee Ann?"

"Where I keep all my secret things, honey," she said. "In the bedroom."

So I followed her there. Knowing it was a bad idea. Followed those long legs and slender hips through beige corridors into a blue velvet bedroom. I left the door open just in case I found the courage to retreat. Lee Ann turned to me with a bright, expectant expression. Her fingers went to the buttons of her white silk blouse and lingered as she said, "I think the first thing we have to do, we have to get over this physical problem we seem to be having."

The little blouse dropped to the floor. I distinctly remember the blouse fluttering down and the way she flicked it away with a bare foot. I think I remember the soft purr of a zipper. Maybe not.

20

WHEN I regained consciousness, I was bound and gagged and locked in the trunk of a moving car. The back of my head felt like a bruised grapefruit and there was a taste of blood in my mouth. Every part of me hurt. Head, neck, shoulders. My ankles hurt where they'd been bound too tight, cutting off circulation. My feet would have hurt if I'd been able to feel them.

Later on, my pride would hurt, when I had the chance to indulge it.

I did not remember being hit. All I could remember was Lee Ann and the falling blouse. Someone must have followed me into the bedroom and smashed me in the back of the head, that much was clear. I settled on Marita as the likely candidate. Who the culprit was didn't really matter, though. Considering my knuckleheaded behavior, I might as well have saved Lee Ann the trouble and tied the ropes myself.

Penny had warned me. "She'll sweet-talk you and then you'll prob'ly fall for her."

Time had no measure, there in stifling dark. After a while the car slowed and there was an abrupt transition. A storm of gravel began to strike the chassis, resonating through the trunk. The bumps threw me up, down, and sideways. The ride over an unpaved surface went on for some time.

Eventually the car stopped. The engine turned off. I heard a car door slam and the sound of footsteps on gravel. Whoever had tied me had done an exemplary job. I was trussed like a turkey, hands behind my back, ankles looped to my wrists. Struggling made the knots tighten. I struggled anyhow. It was something to do.

The footsteps returned. Suddenly the trunk lid popped open and I was blinded by sunlight.

"Well, shit," Jake Bonner said. "What do we do now?"

"We get the girl," Lee Ann said. "We put them together and make it look right. It's the only way."

The trunk lid slammed shut. I heard Jake say, "You think he'll tell us?"

And Lee Ann said, "He'll tell the twins. Where they at?"

"Don't know," Jake said. "Shoulda been here hours ago. You know how Orrin likes to feed them gators."

The footsteps went away and the voices receded. The words they had exchanged stayed with me: "He'll tell the twins" and "Orrin likes to feed them gators" were especially vivid. I twisted and turned and succeeded only in making my hands go numb. Better to concentrate on the gag.

I chewed. I shredded. I spit. Finally part of the gag came lose. I began shouting. Well, screaming is more like it. Wanting to attract attention.

It worked. The lid popped open again.

"Ain't nobody here but me and Lee Ann," Jake said. I caught a glimpse of the jagged skyline of Gator World. He tied on a new gag, tighter than the first, and slammed the trunk shut. That was discouraging. I decided not to waste energy fighting the gag, or the ropes.

"We get the girl. We put them together and make it look right."

Play it anyway you liked and it came back ugly, especially the part about making it look right. I could only assume that Lee Ann intended to make it look like a certain fishing guide was indeed a part-time kidnapper/extortionist, just as Jake had been saying all along.

I had no idea what nasty little scenario they had in mind. It all depended on getting hold of Penny, that much was obvious. Not telling them her whereabouts became, therefore, more important than ever. Not only her life depended on it, but mine as well.

I tried to hold that thought while I waited for the twins.

The next time the trunk lid opened, the sun was low. The stark unfinished framework of the theme park stood out against the fading sky.

"Lee Ann's worried about your hands and feet," Jake said. "We wouldn't want it to look wrong, now, would we?"

I didn't attempt to respond. Questions asked of a gagged man are assumed to be rhetorical. Lee Ann's concern for my swollen extremities was not reassuring. The implication was that she didn't want anything to look wrong on a medical examiner's report.

"Will he fit?" Lee Ann said.

" 'Course he'll fit. These was built to haul bull gators."

Jake got his hands under my arms and tugged me out of the well. Lee Ann grabbed the rope around my ankles. The sudden jolt of pain caused me to scream into the gag as I was dropped into a steel cage. A long, skinny cage on wheels. Narrow enough so my shoulders were jammed. Lee Ann smiled at me as she padlocked the top of the cage. It was a regular hi-how-you-doin' smile, and that chilled me all the more.

After the lock snapped shut, Jake came at me with a knife, poking the blade through the steel mesh. He sliced away the ropes. The pain of blood rushing back into my hands and feet made my eyes water. Through the blur I saw Lee Ann regarding me with the same fixed smile.

"Cut that gag off him," she suggested.

The gag was cut off.

"Where's Penny at?" she asked.

It took a while to work the moisture back into my mouth and throat. "Gone," I said. "Put her on a plane. Evidence with her."

"He's lying," Lee Ann said matter-of-factly. "He's got her hid somewhere. With another of his girlfriends, maybe."

In a way the gator cage was more restricting than the ropes. It was like a long, skinny coffin made of wire mesh. The narrowness kept my hands pinned to my side. There was room to wiggle my swollen toes, but that was about it.

Jake was a little slow on the uptake. He squinted down at me and said, "What evidence?"

"Don't pay him no mind," Lee Ann said. The swamp-side drawl she had struggled so hard to repress had surfaced again. Or maybe it was the special way she had of talking with Cousin Jake. "There's no hard evidence, so he can't have anything that would hold up. Now let's wheel him under cover."

They pushed the cage into a shed building next to

175

the gator pens. The stink of putrefying meat was sickening. Left there to ripen for the alligators, Lee Ann told me. The rotten stuff was oozing from wooden crates that swarmed with flies.

Lee Ann made a face and said, "You all get hungry you can have a few bites."

"I'm a go try them boys again," Jake said, backing out of the shed.

When he was gone, Lee Ann knelt by the cage, running her fingers over the mesh an inch from my face. "Ellis 'n Orrin are mighty pissed at you, honey," she whispered. "You tell me truthful where the girl is, I'll see they don't fun with you too long."

"When did you get into this?" I asked her. "Was it right from the beginning, when Jake persuaded your brothers to dispose of his father-in-law? Or maybe it was your idea from the get-go. Hell, you were only what, fourteen?"

Her eyes were bright. She was alive to the excitement, the proximity of death. "Never you mind about little old Lee Ann. Just tell me where we can lay hands on the girl."

"Don't know," I said. "Left her off at the airport, told her to go anywhere she liked, long as it was out of state. Wherever she ends up, Penny is going straight to the cops, Lee Ann. You better make up your mind. Witness for the prosecution."

She giggled. "You been watching too many movies, honey. Now you gonna tell me true?"

"Told you," I said. "Penny is gone, airborne."

Lee Ann laughed. "Be that way," she said. "Now you rest up, hear? The twins gonna wear you right out."

She left.

From outside came the sound of gators scuttling in

176

their pens. The stench of putrid meat would be making them hungry, if they weren't already. I tried scuttling in my own cage and in time succeeded in working myself to one end. The transportation cages had a hinged lid on either end, the idea being the gators went in one end and were released from the other. I had it in mind that Lee Ann might have neglected to fasten the latch.

No such luck. The latch was locked from the outside. My hands were still weak, but I tried lacing my fingers into the mesh. Maybe I could tear it loose. A dumb idea. I tugged and strained until the wire cut almost to the bone and did absolutely no damage to the gator-proof mesh.

In the pens the tails were starting to thump impatiently. One of the old bulls was roaring. I lay there, nauseated by the smell, and decided that the next time Lee Ann made an appearance I was going to beg for my life.

Never got the chance. The Cullen brothers got to me first. They moved quietly for big men. I didn't know they were in the shed until a bruised, bandaged face loomed over me. Adhesive tape covered his nose and most of one cheek. The eyes were swollen and black, and the mouth, when it opened, showed several stubs of freshly broken teeth.

"Lookee here, Orrin," the face said. "Juss like Annie promise."

Orrin appeared. He had a new sling on his arm and the glazed, sullen look of someone on painkillers. He took a deep breath and shuddered.

" 'Lo dere, mister tough guy," he said.

I thought it better not to respond. Inside, I was trying to distance myself. Shutting down the synapses: I'm not really here. I won't feel a thing. They can't touch me.

Those kinds of thoughts.

"First we go soften you up," Ellis said, staring down at me. "We go soften you up real good."

Orrin had traded in his rifle for a double-barreled shotgun. He handled it well enough with his left hand. He shoved the barrel through the mesh and let it come to rest on my throat. He pulled the trigger. The firing pin clicked.

"Bang," he said softly.

His brother, meantime, had dragged over a crate of the putrid meat. He unlocked the top grate of the cage and jammed a haunch of the meat in beside me. He snapped the lock shut again.

"This gaum be good," he drawled. Then he giggled. Tee-hee-hee.

What they did was drag my cage out into the gator pens. Ellis opened one of the chutes and very soon I had company. A gang of hungry, adolescent gators converged on my cage.

The brothers stood on a catwalk, watching the fun.

"Lookit them pups, they gettin' all agitated."

Indeed they were. Several leathery snouts pressed hard against the mesh, driving the cage sideways as they fought to get at the meat. Maddened by the idea that dinner was so near and yet out of reach. When it became obvious that jaw maneuvers were futile, one of the bigger boys gripped the mesh with his claws and spun me over, slamming the cage to the ground. The same instinctive move he'd have made underwater, when rolling to stun his prey.

It worked. I was stunned. The rugged cage did not yield, however. The haunch of meat remained more or less jammed beside me, a tantalizing appetizer wrapped in high-grade mesh steel. A couple of the beasts backed off, either losing interest or willing to defer to the more aggressive animals. That gave the spinning gator a chance to go into a frenzy. He worked his claws tightly into the mesh and began to roll, slamming the cage with his tail.

The brothers got a real kick out of that. I could hear them braying with laughter. Eventually Ellis got into the pen, armed with a long pole, and drove the gators into an adjacent pen. He dragged my cage back into the shed.

Lee Ann was waiting there. She knelt down and used a slat to knock the mud away from the mesh. She said, "Tell me."

I told her about the airport again.

Lee Ann sighed. "This isn't working. Orrin, you go on and shoot him."

That made Orrin happy. He snapped the breech of his shotgun shut and pressed the barrel against my neck. It went click again. He said, "Bang," again.

"That make you nervous?" Lee Ann wanted to know. "It'd make me nervous. One of these times old Orrin might forget to slip the shell out of the chamber. Look, honey, tell me where the girl is. She won't come to no harm, promise. It's just we need to put the family unit back together, for appearance sake. Tell us where she's at and we'll let you go. Word of honor."

That made Ellis giggle. Lee Ann gave him a look and he stopped, just like that.

"These boys want to do all kinds of terrible things to you, honey," she said in a crooning, soothing voice. "I won't let 'em, if you just only tell me. Please?"

"Okay," I said, and sighed deeply. "I left her with my sister, in Naples."

Lee Ann stroked the mesh with the slat, smiling at

179

me. "You're a pretty good liar," she said. "Might almost go for that sister in Naples. Only thing, Jake had you checked out pretty good, and you don't have any living kin. No brother, no sister."

"Half-sister," I said.

Lee Ann dropped the slat and stood up. She looked at Orrin and said, "Whatever it takes. We'll just have to fix it up later, make it look right."

The brothers looked like they'd just been given an extra-special Christmas present. Lee Ann left without a backward glance.

Orrin pulled his shotgun out of the mesh and knelt beside me. His eyes were like burned-out cinders. "You all can beg some now," he said.

"Penny's in Miami," I said. "She's with a girlfriend of mine, just like Lee Ann suspected."

"Ah don't give a shit where the little brat is at, do you, Ellis?"

"No, suh, bubba. Keep you han' offa that cage now, I'm gon give this boy a poke."

Ellis swung around with the long pole. When it touched the mesh, I knew why the gators had been so eager to run before it. The top was fitted with a cattle prod.

"Ooh-ee, lookit 'im jump. Look like a little old fish on a hook, don't he, Orrin?"

Things got very hazy. At some point they pulled me from the cage and made me take off my sneakers so they could apply the voltage to the bottom of my feet. I tried to lunge at the pole and wrestle it away, but I was weak as a kitten and each succeeding jolt made me weaker. I kept wanting to pass out and the prod kept waking me up again.

It went on for a thousand years or so. I lost the power of speech. I regressed from man to gibbering ape and back into the primeval swamp, until I was a reptile, crawling on my belly. Kicking and shivering as the laughter broke over me in waves.

There came a time when Jake and Lee Ann were in the shed. I was on the ground, trying to sink into it, and they loomed far overhead. Lee Ann had something in her hand. She waved it in my face.

"The Marriott Marco Beach Hotel," she said. "You dumb bastard, you left the brochure in the glove compartment."

I tried to deny that. Something was wrong with my throat, and no words came out.

"Makes sense," Lee Ann said to Jake. "Marco Island makes perfect sense. That's where he was heading all along. To Grandma's house."

"Shee-it," Jake said. "The girl don't hardly know her gramma."

Lee Ann said, "Ellis, Orrin, you all get on up to Marco Island. Check out Irene's place. Ain't nobody there, you go on over the hotel."

The brothers whined and complained. They wanted to keep playing with their new, groveling man-gator. Lee Ann insisted. The argument was settled when a booted foot collided with my forehead. At long last the darkness opened.

21

THEY stored me in the pump house. This was a concrete cube under the water slide, fitted with a steel-plate door. The big pumps that would power the slide hadn't been installed yet. I came to that conclusion in the dark, while tripping over the bolt heads sunk in the concrete floor.

There were no light leaks around the door. That meant it was either sealed with a gasket, or it was night. My head felt stuffed with damp cotton batting. Every part of me hurt. Worst of all the cattle prod had messed up my internal clock. I had no idea how long I'd been out or what time it was.

The hotel!

I'd never thought to check the glove compartment. Even if I had, I might not have noticed the brochure Mutt had left there, or taken care to remove it. There seemed no need at the time. I'd waltzed into the big house in Coral Gables armed with a .38 and the knowledge of the Indigo Springs connection, confident that I could trust to my instincts to bring it off. Instead, it was Lee Ann who made all the right moves. I'd behaved like a dim-witted bull charging a silk blouse.

I was giving that a lot of thought when a bat started squeaking. Then the sound altered pitch and it wasn't a bat; it was a screw twisting. I held my breath and scanned the darkness until I saw a faint rectangle of light forming. In an instant hope flooded through me.

Someone was trying to break me out.

The squeaking stopped. The next sound was metal scratching against concrete. I moved toward the faint light and reached out. My fingers found an indentation in the concrete. I felt a metal grate. It was shifting as someone tried to wrench it loose.

Suddenly the grate popped away and I saw that it had been covering a small ventilation slot. The light was dim and rosy. Dawn or sunset.

"You awake?" Jake Bonner said.

The hope turned brittle and died.

"Got a coffee here," Jake said.

A paper cup appeared in the slot. I picked it up, sniffed the fumes, and drank greedily.

"It's not too late," I said.

He laughed. It was an empty, lonesome sound. "Been too late for a long time now," he said.

"What are you going to do?" I said.

There was a pause. I tried to catch sight of him, but he kept himself away from the opening. "Lee Ann is going to fix things," he said.

"Won't work, Jake. Not this time. They're onto you."

"Lee Ann," he insisted. "She gonna make things right."

I could feel the caffeine sparking in my blood. It wasn't as good as hope, but it gave my heart a reason to keep on beating.

"I told the newspapers," I said.

"Shit on the newspapers," he said. "Shit on the FBI, too. Nobody can't prove it don't happen like we

183

say. I'm a go get us the best lawyers money can buy."

"So you're really going to do it, huh, Jake? Kill your own daughter?"

Another pause. I could hear him shifting his feet. "I don't know about that," he said. "Anyhow, she's Mary Beth's daughter, not mine."

"What?" I said, startled. "You're not Penny's father?"

Jake cleared his throat, speaking softly, as if he didn't want to be overheard. "Mary Beth was knocked up when we run off and got hitched. Some dude she messed with at one of them resort vacations her ma and pa were all the time taking her on."

"Penny doesn't know that."

"No," he said. "Mary Beth wanted it that way."

"Jake," I said, "listen to me. What kind of hold does Lee Ann and her brothers have on you?"

The silence went on for so long I thought he'd gone away. Then there was a deep intake of breath and he said, "I done a bad thing to her, once. A lot more than once. All her kin knew it, too. Where we come from, that means you're obliged."

"Obliged to be an accessory to murder, Jake?"

"Just obliged," he said. "You all wouldn't understand nothing like that. It runs deep."

He was right. I knew that the taboos against incest were deep-rooted, that the practice of it could lead to madness and murder. But I did not really understand what motivated a man like Jake Bonner, or a woman like Lee Ann.

"Come on, Jake," I said. "You can stop it right now. Blame everything on Lee Ann and her brothers. It was the twins who killed Mary Beth's father for you, right? And it was Lee Ann at the wheel when Mary Beth died. You can say it was all her idea. I'll back you up. Just don't let them kill Penny."

His answer was to put the cover back on the ventilation slot and screw it down tight.

Hours went by. I explored every inch of the concrete room and found two more ventilation slots. All were the same size—too small by half, even if I'd been able to back the screws out. Having established escape as an impossibility, I concentrated on finding something I could use as a weapon. A length of re-bar, say, or a fist-sized chunk of concrete. Something to throw, if the door ever opened.

I finally got tired of tripping over the bolts buried in the floor and discovered, to my chagrin, that each had been equipped with a heavy nut and washer. Backing off the nuts was easy. In a matter of moments I had a little hoard of the things. Guesstimated weight about six ounces apiece.

Not exactly my weapon of choice. As ammo for a slingshot it would have been fine, but I had no slingshot, nor the materials to construct one. What I did have was time, and the more of it that went by, the better I felt. Some of the maybes began to even out in my head. Maybe Mutt had gotten the jump of the Cullen brothers. Maybe the FBI had Gator World under surveillance. Maybe Jake Bonner would change his mind.

I put the nuts in my pants pockets and sat down facing the steel door and entertained myself with visions of clear green water. In my daydream a silver-blue bonefish darted through the turtle grass. It was a great big bone, maybe fifteen pounds.

Go for it, Stash old buddy, I thought. You may never get another chance like this.

I shut my eyes tight and concentrated on imagining the cool green water and the beautiful bonefish. He had a jagged blue stripe down his back and a belly as white as platinum. He was waiting out there in the turtle grass. Hungry, ready to strike. I went into the live well and found a crab exactly the right size. Half-dollar size. I slipped the hook through the back edge of the crab's shell and cast it out beyond the tuft of turtle grass where the bonefish was hiding.

It was a lovely vision. I could almost feel the slight motion of the boat, the heat of the sun reflecting off the water. I felt the surge of line leaving the reel as the bonefish ran with the bait. Running so hard and fast it raised a roostertail of spray that made rainbows out of sunlight.

Oh, it was lovely. The best fish I never caught.

Reality was the sound of a pickup truck. Footsteps in the gravel. A fist booming against the steel door. Lee Ann giving orders.

"Orrin, you keep back over there and cover him. Remember his hands are loose." There was a pause and then her voice was closer. "Hey, Stash! You have a nice nap in there, honey? I'm going to pull back on this bolt, then you're going to open it up and come out real polite. Hands on top of your head."

The bolt slid back. Soft light appeared around the door jamb. I cupped one of the iron nuts in my right hand and pulled back on the heavy door with my left. More light spilled in. I pretended to struggle with the door, letting my eyes adjust. When it was now-or-never time, I put both hands on top of my head, the nut cupped in my palm, and shouldered the door far enough open so I could squeeze through.

And stood there blinking into the sunset.

Lee Ann was smiling at me. She was five yards off, holding my .38 with both hands. Orrin stood off to the other side, aiming the double-barreled shotgun with his good hand. She hadn't mentioned Ellis, but there he was, big as life, with matching shotgun. My little plan had relied on there being no more than one weapon pointing at my guts. Lee Ann might miss with the .38 and it was possible that Orrin would have a little trouble swinging his shotgun one-handed, but there was no way Ellis was going to miss from that range. I kept my hands firmly planted on the top of my head.

"Things are coming together," Lee Ann said. "Everything's going to be jess fine."

I shuffled along. It's hard to really appreciate a spectacular sunset when your back is the target of opportunity, but this one was a humdinger. The big sky was a paint box full of blazing pigments that tended to stun the eyes and the senses. It also made it hard to see, at certain angles, and I was trying to figure out how to use that to my advantage as Lee Ann chatted me along.

"Nobody's going to get hurt," she drawled. "We're going to come to a meeting of minds and then shake hands and make up. Right, Ellis?"

"Huh?"

"Nobody gone get hurt, right?"

"Yeah, right."

You could almost believe in Lee Ann. Lighthearted and sincere. Life-affirming. The twins ruined the mood, though. They weren't reading from the same script. They knew how the scene was really going to end and it was too much trouble to pretend otherwise.

The generator kicked in. Strings of temporary lights

began to glow and the half-completed grounds took on an almost festive air. The pickup truck was parked in the area next to the airboat terminal. There were new tires on the El Camino, and a camper top had been bolted on the bed.

Jake was standing next to the truck, wearing his white plantation suit. There was a briefcase on the ground next to his feet. Even in the dimming light you could tell his face was pale and drawn.

"Stop right there," Lee Ann ordered me. "Keep your hands up, just like they are."

I did as I was told.

"Lee Ann," Jake said anxiously, "they brung along Irene. How we gonna make this right with her here?"

"Hush now," Lee Ann said. "Just you give it a little thought, honey. Stash is trading the girl for the ransom money, right? Well, it's the most natural thing in the world you'd ask the girl's gramma for help raising the money. And naturally she'd want to be here, when the girl was cut lose. Honest, hon, this makes it even better."

So much for Lee Ann's reassurances about no one getting hurt. They were planning to stage a payoff and an ensuing shoot-out. When the marl dust settled, several inconvenient persons would be no more. She had it all worked out, right down to the gun that would do most of the killing. Mine.

Armed kidnapper shoots grandmother and child and is in turn cut down. That's how they intended to make it look. It was a nice simple ending. There would be a lot of doubts, but no hostile witnesses to spoil things for the defense.

"The money's here in the briefcase," Jake said hesitantly. "I've got stuff I better take care of at the office."

If Lee Ann was surprised by his shrinking-violet attitude, she didn't let it show. "Sure thing, hon. You go on up there and let us finish our business. Just be ready to make that call when I say so."

Jake left the briefcase on the ground and hurried away like his feet were burning. Plainly he didn't have the stomach to watch what was about to happen. He was willing enough to let it go down, though, once he was out of sight. I wondered if he would stand in his office with his fingers in his ears, waiting for the all-clear from Lee Ann.

She turned to me with a big smile on her pretty face. "You're going to take the money and run, honey. That's the only sensible thing to do. You understand what I'm saying?"

"I believe I do."

" 'Cause the alternative is real unpleasant. You don't help me make it look right, and I'll be obliged to turn the girl over to Ellis and Orrin. You already know how excitable they get."

"You're saying you'll make it quick."

She nodded. "Quick as a little old lightning bug."

"You know how to use that gun?" I said.

That made her smile even more. Lee Ann was getting a kick out of my concern for a quick, clean death.

"I'm no marksman, honey, but I'll be close enough to kiss you all good night."

I nodded. My hands were bathed in sweat. The nut felt like a piece of molten coal under my palm. As if it was glowing. Lee Ann tucked my gun in her waistband and unlocked the back of the pickup.

There were three bodies inside. For one horrible moment I thought the deed had already been done. Then I saw that Mutt was struggling against the ropes. He was tied back to back with Irene. Her eyes rolled, white with fear.

"Ellis, you help me get the girl loose first," Lee Ann said.

Ellis had an objection. "We need Jake," he said.

Lee Ann shook her head. "He's no good to us out here, so just do like I say. You got him covered, right, Orrin?"

"Yes, ma'am," he said, smacking his lips. "I surely do."

Orrin raised his weapon so that both barrels were aiming at my face. His brother put his shotgun on the top of the camper and leaned inside to fetch Penny. She was curled up, as if asleep, or too frightened to open her eyes. While Lee Ann held the child, Ellis used his buckknife to cut her feet loose, then her hands. She still didn't respond. Paralyzed by fear, and who could blame her?

My plan was to duck under the barrel of Orrin's shotgun and throw the heavy nut directly into his face. Then grab the gun and hope I had a chance to use it before Ellis grabbed his, or Lee Ann got the .38 out of her waistband. Figured there was a very slim chance I could pull it off without getting my hair parted permanently.

That wasn't how it happened.

"Carry her over by the airboats," Lee Ann instructed Ellis. "That's where old Stash is going to try and make his escape."

So Ellis picked her up. And Penny exploded out of his arms and clawed at his face, ripping the bandages away. She clamped her teeth, hard, on the end of his broken nose. Blood spurted. Ellis screamed and put his hands over his face. Brother Orrin hesitated, then started to swing the barrel toward them.

I threw the nut with all my might and caught him square in the eye. Both barrels of the shotgun discharged into the ground as he fell.

Ellis, blinded by blood and pain, was groping for his shotgun. Lee Ann was cursing and trying to pull the handgun out of her pants as she warded off a flurry of vicious kicks from Penny. By then Orrin was up on his knees, one eye streaming blood as he attempted to reload his shotgun.

I made a decision. It was probably the wrong decision, but there wasn't a lot of time to think about it. What I did was grab Penny and take to my heels. Just as fast and as far as I could run.

22

A series of small mines detonated behind us. Or that's what it sounded like when Lee Ann discovered that firing a revolver at a rapidly moving target is no easy task. Penny wrapped her arms around me and held on tight. She was light, but not so light I could keep it up for any great distance. We had to find cover, a place to hide.

The nearest structure was the row of geodesic domes enclosing the Night of the Living Swamp exhibition. I darted behind the structure, put Penny down, and forced an exit door. I linked hands with Penny and we went up a ramp to the catwalk that bisected the artificial swamp. The exit door swung shut, cutting off the only source of light. The air was thick with moist heat. I could hear water trickling somewhere in the dark and a few tree frogs complaining about the intrusion.

I tried to remember what the place looked like when Jake had walked me through. We had come in at one end of the building. He had turned to a power grid, thrown a switch, and a temporary generator had been activated, powering the dim lighting and the phony, starlit sky. I wanted to get to that power grid before Lee Ann rallied the troops. Which end of the catwalk? I couldn't remember.

"Heads or tails, Penny," I said. "Choose one."

"Tails."

We jogged forward, stumbling, using the handrail as a guide.

"Are we going to hide?" Penny asked.

In the darkness her young voice was plaintive and uncertain. She was relying on me to sound confident. I faked it.

"We're going to make sure the lights stay off," I replied. "Then we'll find a place to hide."

Tails had been the right choice. I raked my hands over the wall to the left of the sealed entrance doors and found conduits for electrical wires. This was a gingerly business in the dark. If the wiring was in the same state as it had been the day Jake showed me the place, there was nothing to worry about until the generator was activated. If . . .

"Penny," I whispered, "you stand back a little way from me, okay? And don't touch the handrail."

She moved reluctantly away. I located the breaker box. One by one I yanked each circuit breaker free of the grid and hurled it over the rail. Into the dark.

"Penny," I said, "what we're going to do is go over the side together. I think the drop is only a few feet, from this part of the catwalk. You hold on real tight."

She held on. I got both legs over the handrail and pushed off. The drop was more like six or eight feet. It felt like a hundred. I landed feetfirst in something soft and wet, then fell backward into six inches of warm water with Penny on top of me.

I rolled into a sitting position and said, "You think you can walk in this stuff?"

"It's sucking at my feet."

I helped her get her tennis shoes off and kicked

my own away. Barefoot in the dark, in a man-made swamp. What a great hiding place I'd picked.

"Daddy put snakes in here," Penny informed me.

Right at the moment I was more worried about two-legged reptiles. I didn't know if we'd been spotted going into the building, or how long it would take them to organize a search. Not long. Lee Ann was a model of executive efficiency.

The swamp, as I remembered it, was a shallow saw-grass base with a winding creek cut through it. The creek connected the deeper pools that Jake intended to set up as gator holes. The fiberglass reproductions of cypress trees hung with fake moss were situated near the pools. I wanted to find the creek, follow it to a pool, and hide in the thick trees.

"Can you swim?" I asked Penny.

"Just dog-paddle," she said, holding to my hand with a grip that felt like a small steel vise.

I edged through the slippery muck and saw grass, feeling my way forward. Trying to reassure Penny that all would be well even as I expected the doors to burst open and searchlights flood in to expose us.

"Will Gramma be okay?" she wanted to know. "It wasn't her fault, what happened. She went down to the gift shop to get a present for me and they followed her up to our room. Then they pointed a gun at Gramma and Mutt couldn't do anything. He was so mad he almost cried. I could tell."

I damn near slipped, dragging her with me into the creek. At the last possible instant my toes caught in the slick mud. When I got my breath back, I had Penny sit down while I tried to determine how deep it was. Grabbing tufts of saw grass for a handhold, I dropped over the edge and found it was little more than waist-deep, with a gravel bottom. Penny hooked her arms around my neck and got on, piggyback style.

We located the phony cypress trees about five minutes before the first flashlight appeared on the catwalk.

"Get Ellis in here," Lee Ann said. "We'll have to rig up some lights."

She had to be at least a hundred feet away, from the size of the flashlight beam, but the acoustics of the dome structure made it sound like she was hiding behind the dense screen of moss-encrusted cypress with us. A second flashlight joined in, sweeping a feeble beam through the gloom.

"What if he's got a gun?" Jake said.

"Then he'd already have shot us, you damn fool," Lee Ann said. Her tone was still light and bantering. Like she was involved in an interesting game and intended to have fun winning it. "Trust me, he doesn't have a gun. Orrin is sealing the exits." She raised her voice. "Hey, Penny! Honey, tell us where you're at and we'll get you out of this spooky place. Don't believe anything that man is telling you. We'd never hurt you, honey. Honest."

Beside me Penny had clamped her hands over her ears. I could feel her little heart thudding away.

In a lower tone of voice Lee Ann said, "What we need is a bloodhound."

A third flashlight joined them on the catwalk.

"I'm a go kill that little bitch," one of the brothers said.

Lee Ann shushed him and raised her voice again. "Penny, listen to me! This is all a crazy misunderstanding. Like grown-ups have all the time, okay? We thought you'd been kidnapped. We just wanted to get you back, honey. We never meant to hurt you, that's just a great big lie."

It was right about then that something long and slender and snakelike decided to loop itself around my bare ankle. I kicked out, shaking the phony cypress branches.

"Hear that?" Ellis said.

"Is that you, Penny?" Lee Ann called out. "Do it again and we'll find you, sweetheart."

Lee Ann never gave up. She'd be murmuring reassurance even as she slipped your head into the guillotine stocks. Her confidence in her ability to make things right was absolute.

"Orrin," she said, *sotto voce*, "you all help Ellis drag in a string of lights. Hurry."

Orrin didn't hurry all that fast. He seemed to be hurting, from what I could make out in the play of flashlights. Amazing what a little chunk of steel will do when hurled with enough force. Jake gave him a hand looping the lights from the catwalk. Several bulbs got smashed in the process and Orrin cursed as each one popped. Like he was just a wee bit nervous.

"Sumbitch," he complained. "I cain't hardly see. I'm go lose this eye, I don't get a doctor."

"You'll be fine," Lee Ann assured him.

"I'm all busted up," he said. "Cain't you see I'm all busted up?"

His complaints were ignored. The only issue of importance to Lee Ann was the immediate task of finding us. It was no small problem. The Living Swamp exhibit was large and cavernous and had been designed for a dark, atmospheric, junglelike effect. There was plenty of cover. The string of temporary lights hardly illuminated more than the catwalk area, casting wavering shadows on the high dome ceilings. Short of bringing in bloodhounds or a large search party, there was no way of avoiding a yard by yard survey. Or so I thought.

Jake said, "What if we offer him the money?"

Lee Ann laughed. "Come on, Jake, get with the program. This crazy fool doesn't care about money. That's what makes him so dangerous."

But Jake wouldn't be appeased until he'd tried it out himself. He shouted, "Hey, T.D.! There's a hundred thousand bucks in that briefcase. You walk away from all this you can have it! Just let us handle our own problems is all we ask! Hell, we'll even let the girl live with her grandmother, if that's what she really wants! Right, Lee Ann?"

Lee Ann said, "Absolutely. You can live with your gramma, hear that, Penny? She's safe, right out there in the truck. We're real sorry the twins got a little rough with you all. It won't happen again."

Orrin had taken up his shotgun with his good arm. His muttering was indistinct, but plainly he was hurt and angry. Using the handrail to brace the barrel, he fired off both barrels. The explosions were deafening, magnified by the eerie acoustics.

"I'm a go kill 'em," he screamed. "I'm a go set this house afire!"

Lee Ann tore the gun from his hands. The big guy cowered.

"He's delirious," Lee Ann announced. "Pay no attention to the poor man!"

Quite suddenly there was something else that attracted attention. The sound of a low-flying aircraft. Close enough so it might have been buzzing the building. It faded quickly away until it was a mosquito whine in the distance.

"Oh, shit," Jake said. "That sounded like an airboat."

Lee Ann lost her cool. "Ellis! For Chrissake, get your ass in gear. Check it out!"

He was already jogging along the catwalk, headed for the exit. Lee Ann followed him to the door and stood there screaming. Not saying anything in particular, just screaming. It was more frightening than the shotgun blasts. The veneer was blond and beautiful and smart, but under it, where the real Lee Ann lived, was something crazy and ugly. Crazy enough to run a car over Mary Beth because the opportunity presented itself. Crazy enough to decide that a nine-year-old girl who'd overheard a damning conversation was a threat that had to be eliminated.

Ellis returned in a few minutes. He mumbled something.

"What?" Lee Ann demanded. "What did you say?"

"They got loose somehow. They stole an airboat."

"I don't believe this," Lee Ann said.

"We was all for shootin' 'em and gettin' it over," Ellis said sulkily. "You the one said to leave 'em tied up."

So Mutt had done it. He'd gotten away, taking Irene with him. Heading for help. I hugged Penny. The hope and confidence I'd been faking to her began to burn again as a low ember. Go, Mutt.

I hadn't figured on Ellis, though. He had more imagination than I'd given him credit for, and he wanted to make up for letting Mutt and Irene escape.

"Hell," he drawled, "we doan need no *blood*hounds, Annie. We got us some cut little pups'll do jess fine."

All of a sudden it felt like there were snakes nesting in my intestines. Because I knew exactly what

Ellis meant by "pups." His brother, revived by the idea, stopped moaning about his bad eye and his bum arm and set out to help gather the "pups" and drive them into the building.

Lee Ann called out from the catwalk, "Stash, honey. This is going to get ugly real quick."

Jake murmured something and she told him to hush. I could see her in profile, illuminated by the string of bare lightbulbs, and was not happy to observe that she handled a shotgun with a lot more competence than a revolver. She had hunter's instincts. Apparently it ran in the family.

Orrin propped a pair of exit doors open. Night had fallen over the Everglades and a few real stars glittered in the real sky, in contrast to the dots of luminous paint spattered on the dome ceilings. Ellis could be heard outside, whooping it up as he drove the penned-up gators into the building. From my vantage they appeared as low shadows, slithering down the ramp, landing in the fake swamp with an ominous series of splashes.

Orrin was gleeful. He raised his good arm, brandishing the shotgun.

"Bubba, they some hungry," he shouted. "They some hungry!"

It was getting out of Lee Ann's control and she knew it. Staging a cross-fire kidnap scene was one thing. Explaining away this was going to be another level of difficulty altogether, especially with Mutt and Irene on the loose. It just wasn't going to fly, no matter what spin she tried to put on it.

"Keep an eye on them gators, boys," she exhorted. "We just want to flush 'em out, is all."

The twins made noises of agreement, but they had their own agenda. It amounted to bloodlust, and no reasoned arguments can prevail against that. Jake, sensing a disaster in the formation, announced he was leaving the building.

"I'm going out front, keep an eye on the parking lot. Lee Ann, you handle this, understand?"

"I'm handling it," she screamed. Catching herself, she added, "Anybody shows up, you keep 'em away from this building, hear? We'll work it out. It's our word against theirs, remember that."

Jake slunk out of the building. Orrin shut the exit doors and returned to the catwalk with his shotgun. Ellis, armed with the long cattle-prod pole, drove two dozen famished alligators ahead of him. Striding through the saw grass like he was back home in the Big Cypress, beyond the reach of the law. Maybe he thought he was.

There were more splashes as the gators lurched into the man-made creeks. Eager to get away from the cattle prod.

Lee Ann shouted from the catwalk, "Ellis! I want them alive, you hear?"

Be a good boy, I urged him silently, listen to your sister.

23

THE first hint I had that we were not entirely alone in our little hiding place was a low, swishing sort of noise. I shifted position and peered under one of the lower branches, where I had a view of the pool. Jake's idea of a gator hole. Well, it seemed the gators agreed. There was a big fellow cruising in a circle, snout and eye sockets just above the water. The swishing sound was the tail displacing water.

Penny put her lips to my ear and whispered urgently, "Don't be afraid," she said. "Alligators don't like to eat humans."

Penny knew that and I knew that, but did the gator? After a few minutes it lost interest in swimming and crawled up onto the opposite bank. It yawned, showing off its considerable teeth, then snapped its jaws shut and remained pointed in our approximate direction. I wondered if it was sniffing us out. How refined was an alligator's sense of smell, anyhow? And would it be inclined to seek out a human-smelling thing, no matter how hungry it was?

Just a few questions to pass the time. After the initial surge of tail-thrashing activity, the gators seemed to settle into a leisurely exploration of their new environment. Maybe after so many months in the pens they were a bit sluggish, unused to bigger spaces.

Ellis cruised the saw-grass shallows under the catwalk, trying to stir them up. "Come on, you lazy varmints!" And *zap!* would go the cattle prod and another startled gator would escape into the water.

When there was no immediate bloodletting, Lee Ann appeared to calm down. Collecting her thoughts, no doubt, as she tried to scheme her way out of trouble.

"Tell you what," she said to the twins. "We'll leave 'em in here. Just lock the doors like we don't know they're inside. First we handle the problem of Irene escaping and shooting her mouth off. Then we deal with this."

Orrin's answer to that was to fire off another shotgun blast, this time near a spot where several of the gators had gathered.

"Git movin', you," he screamed. "Skedaddle now! Seek 'em out."

Ellis hefted the cattle prod and laughed. Lee Ann responded by stamping her feet. The steel catwalk rumbled like distant thunder. She tried to take the shotgun from Orrin. He refused.

"Leave us be, Annie," he said. "Me 'n El' gone finish this job. Ain't no sumbitch who blew us off a boat be gettin' away alive. So you all make up a good story, hear? Like you always do. Jess leave us be."

I decided that a little pain and suffering did Orrin Cullen good. It made him eloquent, almost. Lee Ann stopped trying to take his gun away. She paced the catwalk with her own shotgun slung expertly underarm. Orrin turned away from her and searched the gloom with his good eye, ready to let go another blast at anything that moved.

For myself, personally, I wouldn't have cared to turn my back on Lee Ann. Blood kin or not.

Ellis, in addition to the cattle prod, had armed himself with a .44 Magnum handgun. It was jammed in his belt right over his crotch, just in case anybody had any doubts about what it stood for. Egged on by his brother, he leveled the handgun and started taking potshots at anything that looked like good cover. Trying to spook us into making a move.

The Magnum sounded like a series of mortar shots detonating haphazardly throughout the building. Penny and I hugged the ground. An upper branch on the cypress split off and dropped into the pool with a splash that sent gators charging in all directions, like ripples from a stone.

I moved slightly, peering through the cover. Ellis was about fifty feet away, with his back to us, reloading the Magnum. A medium-sized gator was slinking up behind him. I cheered silently for the gator.

" 'Hind you," his brother warned.

Ellis turned, hefted the cattle prod, and jolted the animal on its thick neck. It quivered and turned to run away. Ellis followed, snapping the Magnum magazine shut.

"This an outlaw gator, Or! I'm a go teach it a lesson!"

The lesson was fatal. Ellis, laughing as he jogged after the animal, shot it twice as it attempted to launch itself into a nearby pool. There was an immediate increase of tail thrashing in the area as the brother gators lumbered into the deeper water, drawn by the death throes and the blood.

The twins were in high spirits. There was no telling just how far their idea of fun would have gone if Jake hadn't come back into the building on a run.

"Shit, Lee Ann. There's a sheriff car out there and a big guy heading this way."

Ellis reacted as if he'd been electrified by his own cattle prod. He gave up on tormenting the gators and ran, splashing heavily, over to an exit ramp.

"Damn it, Jake," Lee Ann hissed. "I told you to stay out there. Talk at the man."

"What I tell him?" Jake sounded like he was on the verge of hysteria. "What you want me to tell him, huh? How'm I to explain all them shots goin' off soon's he gets out of his car?"

Lee Ann caught sight of Ellis just as he burst through the exit doors. She screamed for him to stop. He wasn't in any mood to listen. A few heartbeats later there was a rapid exchange of gunfire.

"Do something," Jake implored her. "Stop him!"

Lee Ann ran after Ellis. That left Jake and Orrin on the catwalk. Jake with no obvious weapon in hand and Orrin with a busted arm and a bad eye. The odds were unlikely to get any better.

"You stay here and don't move," I told Penny. "Keep still no matter what happens, okay?"

She nodded. I kissed the top of her head and gave her a quick hug. Then I scooted to the end of the covered area, running alongside the back wall. Trying to keep from sinking my bare feet into the muck.

Orrin spotted me and let out a whoop. An instant later a slug slammed into the wall a few yards behind me. I dropped, rolled, came up. Another slug hit the saw grass, exploding mud all over me. I splashed my eyes clean with the tepid water.

"Jake," I shouted. "Jake, do something! It's not too late! You can still choose!"

Orrin was fumbling with the shotgun. It's not an easy thing to fire one-handed, and it's even tougher to reload. He had the breech cracked and was fumbling for the shells. I stood my ground, ready to dive or run if I heard the gun snap shut.

"Come on, Jake! They're closing in!"

I've never been inclined toward cheerleading. Standing barefoot in a reptile-infested swamp fifty feet from a deadly weapon didn't make it any more enjoyable. Jake was hesitating, looking from Orrin to me.

"Sumbitch," Orrin screamed as the shell tumbled from his grasp and rolled along the catwalk. "Gimme a hand here, Jake. We got him, bubba. We got him!"

Orrin bent awkwardly, the gun balanced on his knees, pawing for the shells. Jake didn't move. I heard the breech click shut and started running.

The shot never came. I heard a scream and turned to see Orrin tumbling from the catwalk. There was a tremendous splash as he landed in the pool where his brother had shot the "outlaw" gator. He screamed like a girl. Jake just stood there, looking over the handrail.

I ran for the pool, slogging through the thick mud. The screams were like shards of ice forming in my blood. Orrin was flailing with all his might, trying to ward off the snapping jaws with his broken arm while he tried to haul himself out of the pool with his good hand. There was already a lot of blood in the water. Mostly from the dead gator, I assumed.

He saw me and screamed, "The prod! Pleeese! Oh, God, please!"

Ellis had dropped the long pole in the saw grass. I

was running on instinct, responding to the ungodly screaming. Never mind that he'd been trying to kill me moments before. This was man against reptile. I grabbed the pole and started back.

The scream turned to a gurgle. The gators in the pool were in a frenzy. The last I saw of Orrin was his broken arm. The gator who got that part was having trouble crunching through the cast.

"Jake!" I looked up, expecting to see him on the catwalk. He was gone.

I kept the pole in hand for safety's sake as I slogged back to where I'd left Penny. There was no need. Every gator in the place was in the pool, trying to get a piece of Orrin.

When I got to Penny, her face was glowing and her eyes were as big and bright as silver dollars. She said, "My dad saved you, didn't he?"

"Yes, honey."

No point in explaining that he wasn't her father, not by blood. That could wait for later. We needed to get out of the building fast, before Lee Ann and Ellis got it in mind to make a stand there—or take hostages.

The night was sultry, starlit, and charged with the sharp odor of exploded cordite. Somewhere a police radio was blaring static. Blue and red lights flickered on bare concrete. A gunshot rang out, echoing off steel. The echoes and reflected lights made it tough to get a fix on location; it seemed to come from everywhere.

With Penny close at my side, we kept to the shadows, ready to duck behind the concrete abutments of the unfinished water slide. The pilings staggered off into the dark like figments in a De Chirico nightscape. The gravel underfoot was sharp and cutting. I hardly felt it. I was sickened by a strange sensation of ecstasy.

There is nothing like the proximity of violent death to make you feel intensely alive. Nothing that feels quite so wrong. I'd been knocked out, bound and gagged, made insensible with fear, beaten unconscious. And yet Orrin's death had left my blood sparking, my batteries fully charged. I had the idea—and knew how dangerous it was—that bullets couldn't touch me.

I was crazy, for just a little while. I was inflated, lighter than air. What tethered me to earth was the hand of a brave child.

The giddiness began to dissipate when we got within visual range of the parking lot. The profusion of blinking lights and the radio static were coming from a single vehicle. The driver's door was open and the headlights were flashing.

As I squinted, trying to make out the county emblem on the door, the windshield exploded.

From somewhere in the dark Ellis screamed, "You dead, you sumbitch! Dead!"

There was answering fire from under the vehicle. Bright muzzle flashes. Not dead then, just pinned down. Two other vehicles were parked nearby. Jake's metallic-red Porsche and the rental car that I had driven to Coral Gables and that Lee Ann had used to transport me back to the park. The trunk lid of the rental car was open. I wondered what the chance was of finding keys in either ignition and decided it was about nil.

The other thing I wondered was whether the lawman under the cruiser had had a chance to use the radio to call in help before Ellis pinned him down.

The thing was squawking high-volume static now, not a clear channel. I had no idea what that might indicate, if anything.

There was another matter of some concern. The location of Lee Ann and Jake. I couldn't see Ellis, but from the way he was shooting, he was using the ticket booths as cover and firing his handgun with the kind of confidence that meant he had a box or two of cartridges in his possession. As for Jake, I suspected he was keeping his head down, or trying to engineer an escape, but I couldn't even guess at Lee Ann's state of mind. Maybe she'd thrown in with Ellis and was working her way around to ambush the sheriff from behind. I thought I saw a figure moving out there, near the Porsche, but I couldn't be sure. The flashing lights made it look like everything was moving.

"Is Gramma really okay?" Penny wanted to know. Each time a shot was fired she jumped. Just like me.

"She got away with Mutt. She'll be fine," I said, knowing full well it was an assumption based on faith, not facts.

I expected that if help was going to arrive it would be in the form of more sheriff's cruisers, or possibly the highway patrol. I hadn't expected an airboat driven by a maniac.

The drone of it tickled the air for a while before it came into view. There was just enough starlight glinting off the spray the boat kicked up to reveal that it was racing right alongside the access road at a speed that sent it airborne each time it hit a tuft of saw grass. The drone was accompanied by a strange, bloodcurdling noise. As it got closer, I could see there was a madman on the stick, howling a war cry at the top of his lungs.

The airboat skidded into a wide turn, losing some forward speed and nearly capsizing. Then it came ashore at full throttle, tearing its hull to pieces. I watched, dazed, as a tall, bare-chested, bald-headed maniac launched himself out of the wreckage. He had a deer rifle slung over his naked shoulders and he charged through the parking lot like he was hitting the beach at Normandy.

I stood up and yelled, "Mutt! Over here, you crazy bastard! Keep your head down!"

24

MUTT changed direction, searching for us in the dark. After a broken-field run across the parking lot he arrived in a splash of marl dust and gravel. He gasped and looked up with his eyes so big and bright they might have been carved into a pumpkin.

"Man, oh, man," he panted, hugging both of us tightly. "Man, oh, man, I thought sure you was goners."

He was out of breath, as hyped up and chattery as a speed freak. His explanation of how he and Irene had managed to escape was disjointed, but it went something like this. After much effort they had severed the ropes by rubbing their tied-together ankles against the tailgate. The airboat had been right there for the taking. Mutt had had no chart, no real idea of where he was, save that it was somewhere in the Everglades. When Irene spotted moving lights, Mutt had steered for them, goosing the airboat for all it was worth. Making maybe fifty miles per, but who could tell at night? Anyhow they'd caught up to the highway in no time. It was, no great surprise, the Tamiami Trail. He ran east for a few miles until they saw what Mutt described as a "gathering of lights."

"Truck stop," he said. "We run in. Irene went to the phone to call the cops. I begged a deer rifle off one of them truckers and left at a run."

"Where's Gramma now?" Penny wanted to know.

"Left her there, child. She was so wild to save you I thought she might do something crazy, you know?"

Unlike Mutt, the tower of reason, who'd come ashore at full scream, howling like a banshee.

"That was to distract 'em," he explained. "Old Seminole tactic."

"Sure glad to see you, Chief."

"Yeah, well, I got snookered by them two apes. Shoulda never let Irene go out of the room on her own. Felt like a damn fool, and nearly a *dead* damn fool."

There were items of more pressing importance than assigning blame. Like what to do about the standoff that had developed in the parking lot. It was reasonable to assume that the lone sheriff had responded to a radio call from a dispatcher alerted by Irene. He must have been nearby to have arrived before Mutt and the airboat. If he was out of contact with his dispatcher, as the static indicated, then it was only a matter of time before backup arrived. Exactly how long that might be was anybody's guess.

Mutt had a bright idea. "What we need is some light on the situation," he said.

He handed me the deer rifle and sprinted back into the parking lot before I could restrain him. In his Key West bait shack Mutt moves with all the deliberate speed of a tortoise immersed in tar—under fire he ran like an NFL wide receiver. It is amazing what a dose of adrenaline will do for the human body. Mutt dashed out to the rental car, reached into the open trunk, grabbed something, and made it back unscathed. It's possible that Ellis Cullen, concentrating his fire on the cruiser, never even saw him.

"What the hell was that all about, Mutt?"

"Flares," he said, showing off the package. "They told me when I rented the thing there was road flares in the trunk."

"I get it," I said. "You're going to distract the gunman by going out there and changing a tire. It's brilliant. Why didn't I think of it?"

Mutt gave me his most sorrowful look. Basset hounds appear cheerful in comparison. "Know what, T.D.? You suffer from a lack of imagination. I mean it."

"Just kidding, Mutt. I'll throw the flares. You see if you can get a bead on Ellis. And don't forget Lee Ann and Jake are out there somewhere, and Lee Ann's got my gun, and a shotgun, and God knows what else."

The concrete ticket booths from which Ellis was directing his siege were laid out like highway toll booths, covered by a flat, gravel-drainage roof with wide overhangs. The staging the roofers had set up was still partly in place. I tucked the flares in my back pocket and worked my way over to the staging. Waiting for a burst of gunfire to cover any noise I might make. I didn't have to wait long. There was a .38-caliber pop from under the cruiser and a barrage of return fire from Cullen's .44.

The staging rattled and squeaked. To me it was louder than the handguns. I lay flat on the rooftop, waiting to see how Ellis would react. Another barrage of shots convinced me he was still focused on the cop cruiser. The .44 cannon had a muzzle flash like a rocket launcher, white and hot. It was a pretty good indication of what booth he was using as cover. I crawled along the roof edge until I was over the source of the muzzle flashes.

It was now or never. I had to assume that Mutt was in position with the deer rifle. I got the flares out and laid them a handbreadth apart on the roof. Igniting them was accomplished by peeling off a friction cover and striking it against the end. The idea was to get them going and drop them over the edge before Ellis had a chance to react.

The first two flares ignited easily. They bounced, sizzling, to the ground. Glowing hot and bright and red. Merry Christmas, Mr. Cullen. The third was stubborn and I'd just decided to give up on it when Ellis bellowed directly below me. A chunk of the roof where I was sitting exploded. Then another. I scrambled back, keeping low. Another chunk of roof exploded upward. All of this happened in a few heartbeats, but it was more than enough time to reconsider the wisdom of dropping road flares on the owner of a hand-held cannon.

Come on, Mutt.

There were muzzle flashes from under the cruiser, zeroing in on the light of the flares. Ellis reacted by rolling out of the ticket booth. From a seated position on the ground he fired at the spot where I had been crouching only moments before. I hugged the roof, trying to look like a lump of asphalt and gravel.

I'm not sure what the big man had in mind when he went for one of the sputtering flares. He reared back, as if intending to throw it up on the roof. Giving me a taste of my own medicine, maybe. It never left his fist. I saw him jerk, then heard the rifle shot. Ellis turned slowly, holding the flare aloft. The rifle cracked again. He held the Statue of Liberty pose until the flare burned into his fist. Then he seemed to wilt, as if melting from the feet up. The flare was still in his fist when he hit the ground. In the peculiar posture death gave him it looked like he was trying to eat a blazing red ice-cream cone.

I came down off the roof and-picked the flare out his hand. This was a very dumb move, since I was barefoot. I was still hopping around when Mutt shouted from the cruiser.

"Come on over here 'n gimme a hand."

I hobbled over to the cruiser. All four tires were flat. The sedan had more holes than a Richard Nixon alibi. Penny darted out from the shadows and threw her arms around my waist.

"You okay?" I asked.

"Aye, aye, Captain."

"Hey, the man's stuck under his vehicle," Mutt said. "You take a hold the bumper, I'll pull him out."

I did the best I could, but lifting cop cruisers is something best attempted early in the day, before you've been through electro-convulsive therapy with a cattle prod. Tyrone Whiddon, the Monroe County sheriff, left a few bits of himself on the underside of the chassis. The final result, after they patched him up, was an extra cleft in his chin. On the whole I think it improved his appearance, if not his sweet disposition.

When Mutt finally dragged him clear of the car, I let the bumper down and sagged right along with it.

" 'Lo, Tyrone," I said. "You're in the wrong county."

Whiddon crawled to his feet and slipped his pearl-handled revolvers into his holster with shaky hands. "You Penny Bonner?" he said to Penny.

She turned to me and asked, in a small voice, "What should I say?"

"Tell him the truth," I said. "See what happens."

"Yes, sir," she said, looking up at the tall, poker-faced lawman. "I am."

Whiddon nodded, turned to me, and said, "You're T. D. Stash, have I got that right?"

I decided to stick with my own advice. "Yes, sir," I said. "I am."

"Well, then," he drawled, "you're under arrest."

So much for the truth.

"Wait just a damn minute, Mr. Sheriff," Mutt interrupted. "You mean to say you're not here responding to a call from a Tamiami truck stop?"

Whiddon shook his grizzly, angular head. "Nope," he said.

"Son of a bitch," Mutt said. "What happened to Irene and all them lawmen she was calling?"

What had happened was an unrelated traffic accident that had shut down two lanes of the Tamiami Trail, although we didn't learn the particulars until later. When the highway patrol finally did arrive, they came full bore down the dirt access road, lights and sirens blazing. For all that, I don't think they were any more effective than Mutt's banshee battle cry.

Irene leapt out of the lead vehicle. She had Penny wrapped in her arms before her feet hardly touched the ground. Within minutes the place was swarming with khaki uniforms.

"Tyrone," I said, "how was it you knew we were here if you didn't get it off the radio dispatcher?"

He said, "Call me Sheriff Whiddon."

I repeated the question as instructed. Glad to know he was grateful for having his life saved, if not all of his skin.

"Fella phoned in a tip. Anonymous. Said you'd bitten off more than you could chew and he was afraid you might come to harm. Suggested I locate Jake Bonner and you'd be somewhere in the vicinity."

"This fella," I said, "he sound like a newspaper type of fella?"

"Could be."

A highway-patrolman commander arrived, holding a notebook and a flashlight. He was built to typical patrol dimensions and didn't seem inclined to defer to a sheriff who was thirty miles over the county line.

"There's a death-by-gunshot report has to be filled out. Also we'd like to have a few words with Jake Bonner," he said. "After we get through with him, the FBI has sloppy seconds. You know where he's at?"

"Thought I saw him near the Porsche. Can't be sure."

Jake wasn't near the Porsche, he was in it. Behind the wheel with the key in the ignition and a round red hole in his forehead. A thread of blood trickled from his nose. In the glare of the flashlights he looked annoyed, as if embarrassed to be caught without a handkerchief.

Sheriff Whiddon, determined to impress the highway patrol somehow, frog-marched me over to the crime scene and made me take a close look at Jake.

"You know anything about this?" he demanded.

I jerked loose of his grasp. My shirt got a little frayed in the process and I decided to punish Tyrone by addressing my answer to the young patrol commander. "I can guess what happened," I said. "Mr. Bonner wanted to get away, leaving his troubles behind, and Mrs. Bonner responded by expressing her disappointment. She may or may not have a .38 Smith and Wesson in her possession. The weapon is registered in my name."

The commander looked at the cooling husk of Jake Bonner and sighed. "I hate domestic calls. Everything gets so complicated. Okay, buster," he said to me, "tell me what's going on, and no bullshit."

I told him. I think he believed about half of it. Enough so that he instructed his men to search the grounds for a blond female.

Thirty minutes later they found Lee Ann hiding in one of the airboats. I wasn't there to see it, but the patrolmen said she ran like a gazelle. They caught up with her at the water's edge, where she tried to throw my Smith & Wesson into the Everglades. The briefcase full of cash was a few yards away.

"We put the cuffs on her and she just laughed," an incredulous patrolman told his commander. "Like it was all a big joke."

Lee Ann was still grinning when they put her in the cruiser. She wore the handcuffs like a pair of silver bracelets. Two of her brothers were dead, her husband was dead, yet none of it touched her. When she saw me, she stuck out her tongue and smirked, like she'd been caught stealing cookies and so what?

"I don't care what anybody says," Lee Ann said. "It's not my fault."

25

ONE day in October we sealed Connie Geiger's ashes in a lime-green flower urn she'd made with her own hands, and carried it to the Key West cemetery, to a tiny plot not far from the monument to the USS *Maine*. We made a kind of weird and sad Key West thing of it, which Connie would have appreciated. Mutt attended, of course, in the sky-blue blazer and a new panama hat like the one he'd worn to the beach at Marco Island. He'd given a lot of thought as to the gesture he wanted to make. The result was a wicker bird cage he hugged to his chest until the ceremony concluded. Inside the cage Connie's favorite bird, a solitary verio, fluffed its yellow-tipped feathers and sang. No one knew where or how he'd captured the bird and he did not care to explain.

Most everyone who had loved Connie attended. Friends, lovers, craftspeople who knew the soul of her work. There were schoolteachers and bartenders and fishermen and a stripper from the Pirate's Den. Lily Cashman showed up, lawyer-late, hiding her red-rimmed eyes behind dark glasses. Even barefoot Fletcher Brown cleaned himself up and came with his conch horn, his white ponytail smelling of aloe-scented shampoo.

Anyone who cared to said a few words. Nelson

Kerry was the most eloquent. He placed a pink hibiscus blossom on the urn and spoke for all of us when he said, "Connie liked to make beautiful things for people to have and to hold and to use in their daily lives. The very last beautiful thing she did was save the life of a child. We'll miss Connie. That doesn't mean we love her less."

Then Fletcher Brown played a few mournful notes on his conch shell and Penny opened the bird cage and the little verio flew out and perched on a nearby monument. It was still singing when we left the sun-drenched cemetery.

Cayo Hueso, island of bones.

That was three years ago. Since then Lee Ann has been tried twice for the murder of Jake Bonner. The first conviction was overturned on appeal and the second trial ended without judgment, when a juror stood up in court and shouted that Jesus had commanded that Lee Ann be hung by her pretty neck until dead dead dead. The only thing that got hung was the jury. Lee Ann is now out on bail while the Dade County prosecutors try to put together another case, possibly involving the death of Mary Beth Bonner. If that fails to stick, the D.A. swears he'll try her for assault and attempted murder of yours truly, if I'm willing to testify. I'm willing enough, but have no illusions about who will look prettier or more convincing to a jury.

Mostly I try not to think about Lee Ann, or Anna Lee, or whatever she calls herself these days. I do, however, keep the bolt latched on the back door, and I go out of my way to avoid large reptiles.

Speaking of which, the Gator World project was taken over by Jake Bonner's creditors. They got the injunction lifted and completed the first phases of construction. The place opened recently under a different name. According to the feature Stan Horn wrote for the *Miami Herald*, business is booming. Suckers aren't born in this part of the world, but so long as Miami International remains open, they'll keep arriving every few minutes.

Some things go wrong, like Lee Ann and the trial. Other things go right.

Just last week Penny and Irene came down for their semiannual visit to Key West. Penny is twelve now, long-legged and gawky beautiful. She still sees a child therapist, and either the therapy is working or—my theory—she's just tough enough to heal on her own. Irene is frequently mistaken for her mother, which please them both immensely. Irene and I have discussed trying to locate her real father, but we keep putting off the decision. One of these days Penny can decide.

We did our usual thing that day, which is to pack up a picnic lunch and take *Bushwhacked* out to the flats east of Ballast Key, where we throw lures at whatever fish happen by, and keep our eyes peeled for green turtles. Mostly we sit and drift and remark on the changing colors of the Gulf. Lazy, the way I like it.

I haven't really gotten used to the idea that Penny is growing up so fast. The child is mother to the emerging woman, though, and she has never lost interest in the small creatures of the land and the sea. During our most recent excursion Penny announced that after long and careful consideration she had decided what she was going to do when she grew up. In the bow of *Bushwhacked* she hugged her bare freckled knees and said, "I'm going to save the Everglades, that's what I'm going to do."

"All by yourself?" I asked.

"Don't be silly," she said, her eyes glowing like green lanterns. "I'm going to need lots of help. It will take years and years, but we'll do it. You'll see."

The thing is, I believe her.

About the Author

Before turning to fiction, **W. R. Philbrick** covered the waterfront as a longshoreman and later as a boatbuilder. From time to time he has lived and worked in the Florida Keys, most recently aboard the *Caribaya*, a vessel he designed and built.